Praise for Val McDermid

'No one can tell a story like she can'
Daily Express

'A master craftswoman at work'
Observer

'There aren't many to touch her for insight into the
minds of hunter and hunted'
Susan Hill

'One of today's most accomplished crime writers'
Literary Review

'As good a psychological thriller as it is
possible to get'
Sunday Express

'It grabs the reader by the throat and never lets go'
Daily Mail

'The queen of crime is still at the top of her game'
Independent

By Val McDermid

A Place of Execution
Killing the Shadows
The Grave Tattoo
Trick of the Dark
The Vanishing Point

ALLIE BURNS NOVELS

1979
1989

LINDSAY GORDON NOVELS

Report for Murder
Common Murder
Final Edition
Union Jack
Booked for Murder
Hostage to Murder

KAREN PIRIE NOVELS

The Distant Echo
A Darker Domain
The Skeleton Road
Out of Bounds
Broken Ground
Still Life

TONY HILL/CAROL JORDAN NOVELS

The Mermaids Singing
The Wire in the Blood
The Last Temptation
The Torment of Others
Beneath the Bleeding
Fever of the Bone
The Retribution
Cross and Burn
Splinter the Silence
Insidious Intent
How the Dead Speak

KATE BRANNIGAN NOVELS

Dead Beat
Kick Back
Crack Down
Clean Break
Blue Genes
Star Struck

SHORT STORY COLLECTIONS

The Writing on the Wall
Stranded
Christmas is Murder (ebook only)
Gunpowder Plots (ebook only)

NON-FICTION

A Suitable Job for a Woman
Forensics
My Scotland

Val McDermid

CHRISTMAS IS MURDER

SPHERE

SPHERE

First published in Great Britain in 2020 by Sphere
This paperback edition published by Sphere in 2022

5 7 9 10 8 6

'Happy Holidays' first appeared in *Exit Wounds* (Titan, 2019); A Wife in a Million' first appeared in *Reader, I Murdered Him* (The Women's Press, 1989); 'A Traditional Christmas' first appeared in *Reader, I Murdered Him Too* (The Women's Press, 1994); 'Long Black Veil' first appeared in *Crime + Music* (Three Rooms Press, 2016); 'The Girl Who Killed Santa Claus' first appeared in *News of the World* magazine, 2000; 'Ancient and Modern' first appeared as 'The Hermit's Castle' in *Bloody Scotland* (Pegasus Books, 2017); 'The Devil's Share' first appeared in *My Scotland* (Little, Brown, 2019); 'Ghost Writer' first appeared in *Good Housekeeping*, 2013; 'White Nights, Black Magic' first appeared in *Crime in the City* (Do-Not Press, 2002); 'Heartburn' first appeared in *Northern Blood 2* (Flambard Press, 1995); 'Four Calling Birds' first appeared in *12 Days* (Virago, 2004).

A CIP catalogue record for this book is available from the British Library.

ISBN 978-0-7515-8176-8

Typeset in Meridien by M Rules
Printed and bound in the UK by Clays Ltd, Elcograf S.p.A.

Papers used by Sphere are from well-managed forests
and other responsible sources.

Sphere
An imprint of
Little, Brown Book Group
Carmelite House
50 Victoria Embankment
London EC4Y 0DZ

An Hachette UK Company
www.hachette.co.uk

www.littlebrown.co.uk

Val McDermid is an international number one best-selling author whose books have been translated into more than forty languages and sold over eighteen million copies. Her multi-award-winning series and standalone novels have been adapted for TV and radio, most notably the *Wire in the Blood* series featuring clinical psychologist Dr Tony Hill and DCI Carol Jordan. An ITV adaptation of the Karen Pirie series, featuring a Scottish cold case detective, is underway.

Val was chair of the Wellcome Book Prize in 2017 and has served as a judge for both the Women's Prize for Fiction and the 2018 Man Booker Prize. She is the recipient of six honorary doctorates and is an Honorary Fellow of St Hilda's College, Oxford. She is a visiting professor in the Centre of Irish and Scottish Studies at the University of Otago in New Zealand. Among her many awards are the CWA Diamond Dagger recognising lifetime achievement and the Theakston's Old Peculier award for Outstanding Contribution to Crime Writing. Val is also an experienced broadcaster and much-sought-after columnist and commentator across print media.

Contents

HAPPY HOLIDAYS

I

A chrysanthemum burst of colour flooded the sky. 'Oooh,' said the man, his blue eyes sparking with reflected light.

'Aaah,' said the woman, managing to invest the single syllable with irony and good humour. Her shaggy blonde hair picked up colour from the fireworks, giving her a fibre-optic punk look at odds with the conservative cut of her coat and trousers.

'I've always loved fireworks.'

'Must be the repressed arsonist in you.'

Dr Tony Hill, clinical psychologist and criminal profiler, pulled a rueful face. 'You've got me bang to rights, guv.' He checked out the smile on her face. 'Admit it, though. You love Bonfire Night too.' A scatter of green and red tracer raced across the sky, burning after-images inside his eyelids.

DCI Carol Jordan snorted. 'Nothing like it. Kids shoving bangers through people's letter boxes, drunks sticking lit fireworks up their backsides, nutters throwing bricks when the fire engines turn up to deal with bonfires that've gone out of control? Best night of the year for us.'

Tony shook his head, refusing to give in to her sarcasm. 'It's been a long time since you had to deal with rubbish like that. It's only the quality villains you have to bother with these days.'

As if summoned by his words, Carol's phone burst into life. 'Terrific,' she groaned, turning away and jamming a finger into her free ear. 'Sergeant Devine. What have you got?'

Tony tuned out the phone call, giving the fireworks his full attention. Moments later, he felt her touch on his arm. 'I have to go.'

'You need me?'

'I'm not sure. It wouldn't hurt.'

If it didn't hurt, it would be the first time. Tony followed Carol back to her car, the sky hissing and fizzing behind him.

The smell of cooked human flesh was unforgettable and unambiguous. Sweet and cloying, it always seemed to coat the inside of Carol's nostrils for days, apparently lingering long after it should have been nothing more than a memory. She wrinkled her nose in disgust and surveyed the grisly scene.

It wasn't a big bonfire, but it had gone up like a torch. Whoever had built it had set it in the corner of a fallow field, close to a gate but out of sight of the road. The evening's light breeze had been enough to send a drift of sparks into the hedgerow and the resulting blaze had brought a fire crew to the scene. Job done, they'd checked the wet smoking heap of debris and discovered the source of the smell overwhelming even the fuel that had been used as an accelerant.

As Tony prowled round the fringes of what was clearly the scene of a worse crime than arson, Carol consulted the lead fire officer. 'It wouldn't have taken long to get hold,' he said. 'From the smell, I think he used a mixture of accelerants – petrol, acetone, whatever. The sort of stuff you'd have lying around your garage.'

Tony stared at the remains, frowning. He turned and called to the fire officer. 'The body – did it start off in the middle like that?'

'You mean, was the bonfire built round it?'

Tony nodded. 'Exactly.'

'No. You can see from the way the wood's collapsed around it. It started off on top of the fire.'

'Like a guy.' It wasn't a question; the fireman's answer had clearly confirmed what Tony already thought. He looked at Carol. 'You do need me.'

Tony smashed the ball back over the net, narrowly missing the return when his doorbell rang. He tossed the Wii control on to the sofa and went to the door. 'We've got the post-mortem and some preliminary forensics,' Carol walked in, not waiting for an invitation. 'I thought you'd want to take a look.' She passed him a file.

'There's an open bottle of wine in the fridge,' Tony said, already scanning the papers and feeling his way into an armchair. As he read, Carol disappeared into the kitchen, returning with two glasses. She placed one on the table by Tony's chair and settled opposite him on the sofa, watching the muscles in his face tighten as he read.

It didn't make for comfortable reading. A male between twenty-five and forty, the victim had been alive when he'd been put on the bonfire. Smoke inhalation had killed him, but he'd have suffered tremendous pain before the release of death. He'd been bound hand and foot with wire and his mouth had been sealed by some sort of adhesive tape. For a moment, Tony allowed himself to imagine how terrifying an ordeal it must have been and how much pleasure it had given the killer. But only for a moment. 'No ID?' he said.

'We think he's Jonathan Meadows. His girlfriend reported him missing the morning after. We're waiting for confirmation from dental records.'

'And what do we know about Jonathan Meadows?'

'He's twenty-six, a garage mechanic. Lives with his girlfriend in a flat in Moorside—'

'Moorside? That's a long way from where he died.'

Carol nodded. 'Right across town. He left work at the usual time. He told his girlfriend and his mates at work that he was going to the gym. He usually went three or four times a week, but he never showed up that night.'

'So somewhere between – what, six and eight o'clock? – he met someone who overpowered him, bound and gagged him, stuck him on top of a bonfire and set fire to him?'

'That's about the size of it. Anything strike you?'

'That's not easy, carrying out something like that.' Tony flicked through the few sheets of paper again. His mind raced through the possibilities, exploring the message of the crime, trying to make a narrative from the bare bones in front of him. 'He's a very low-risk victim,' he said. 'When young men like him die violently, it's not usually like this. A pub brawl, a fight over a woman, a turf war over drugs or prostitution, yes. But not this kind of premeditated thing. If he was just a random victim, if anyone would do, it's more likely to be a homeless person, a drunk staggering home last thing, someone vulnerable. Not someone with a job, a partner, a life.'

'You think it's personal?'

'Hard to say until we know a lot more about Jonathan Meadows.' He tapped the scene-of-crime report. 'There doesn't seem to be much in the way of forensics at the scene.'

'There's a pull-in by the gate to the field. It's tar-macked, so no convenient tyre tracks. There's a few footprints, but they're pretty indistinct. The SOCOs think he was wearing some sort of covering over his shoes. Just like the ones we use to preserve the crime scene.' Carol pulled a face to emphasise the irony. 'No convenient cigarette ends, Coke cans or used condoms.'

Tony put down the file and drank some wine. 'I don't think he's a beginner. It's too well executed. I think he's done this before. At least once.'

Carol shook her head. 'I checked the database. Nothing like this anywhere in the UK in the last five years.'

That, he thought, was why she needed him. She thought in straight lines, which was a useful attribute in a cop, since, however much they might like to believe otherwise, that was how most criminals thought. But years of training and experience had honed his own corkscrew mind till he could see nothing but hidden agendas stretching backwards like the images in an infinity mirror. 'That's because you were looking for a burning,' he said.

Carol looked at him as if he'd lost it. 'Well, duh,' she said. 'That's because the victim was burned.'

He jumped to his feet and began pacing. 'Forget the fire. That's irrelevant. Look for low-risk victims who were restrained with wire and gagged with adhesive tape. The fire is not what this is about. That's just window dressing, Carol.'

Carol tapped the pile of paper on her desk with the end of her pen. Sometimes it was hard not to credit Tony with psychic powers. He'd said there would be at least one other victim, and it looked as if he'd been right. Trawling the databases with a different set of parameters had taken Carol's IT specialist a few days. But she'd finally come up with a second case that fit the bill.

The body of Tina Chapman, a thirty-seven-year-old teacher from Leeds, had been found in the Leeds–Liverpool canal a few days before Jonathan Meadows' murder. A routine dredging had snagged something unexpected and further examination had produced a grisly finding. She'd been gagged with duct tape, bound hand and foot with wire, tethered to a wooden chair weighted with a cement block and thrown in. She'd been alive when she went into the water. Cause of death: drowning.

A single parent, she'd been reported missing by her thirteen-year-old son. She'd left work at the usual time, according to colleagues. Her son thought she'd said she was going to the supermarket on her way home, but neither her credit card nor her store loyalty card had been used.

Carol had spoken to the Senior Investigating Officer in charge of the case. He'd admitted they were struggling. 'We only found her car a couple of days ago in the car park of a hotel about half a mile from the supermarket her son said she used. It was parked down the end, in a dark corner out of range of their CCTV cameras. No bloody idea what she was doing down there. And no joy from forensics so far.'

'Anybody in the frame?'

His weary sigh reminded her of cases she'd struggled with over the years. 'It's not looking good, to be honest. There was a boyfriend, but they split up about six months ago. Nobody else involved, it just ran out of road. Quite amicable, apparently. The boyfriend still takes the lad to the rugby. Not a scrap of motive.'

'And that's it?' Carol was beginning to share his frustration. 'What about the boy's real father?'

'Well, he wasn't what you'd call any kind of father. He walked out on them when the lad was a matter of months old.'

Carol wasn't quite ready to let go the straw she'd grasped. 'He might have come round to the idea of having some contact with the boy.'

'I doubt it. He died in the Boxing Day tsunami back in '04. So we're back to square one and not a bloody thing to go at.'

Carol still couldn't accept she'd reached the end of the road. 'What about her colleagues? Any problems there?'

She could practically hear the shrug. 'Not that they're letting on about. Nobody's got a bad word to say about Tina, and I don't think they're just speaking well of the dead. She's been working there for four years and doesn't seem to have caused a ripple with other staff or parents. I can't say I share your notion that this has got anything to do with your body, but I tell you, if you come up with anything that makes sense of this, I'll buy you a very large drink.'

Making sense of things was what Bradfield Police paid Tony for. But sometimes it was easier than others. This was not one of those occasions. Carol had dropped off the case files on Jonathan Meadows and Tina Chapman at Bradfield Moor, the secure hospital where he spent his days among the criminally insane, a clientele whose personal idiosyncrasies he did not always find easy to distinguish from the population at large.

Two victims, linked by their unlikelihood. There was no evidence that their paths had ever crossed. They lived thirty miles apart. Carol's team had already established that Tina Chapman did not have her car serviced at the garage where Jonathan Meadows worked. He'd never attended a school where she'd taught. They had no apparent common interests. Anyone other than Tony might have been reluctant to forge any link between the two cases. Carol had pointed that out earlier, acknowledging that her counterpart in Leeds was far from convinced there was a connection. Tony's instincts said otherwise.

As he read, he made notes. *Water. Fire. Four elements?* It was a possibility, but admitting it took him no further forward. If the killer was opting for murder methods that mirrored fire, water, earth and air, what did it mean? And why did it apply to those particular victims? Tina Chapman was a French teacher. What had that to do with water? And how was a garage mechanic connected to fire? No, unless he could find more convincing connective tissue, the four elements theory wasn't going anywhere.

He studied the file again, spreading the papers across the living room floor so he could see all the information simultaneously. And this time, something much more interesting caught his attention.

Carol stared at the two pieces of paper, wondering what she was supposed to see. 'What am I looking for?' she said.

'The dates,' Tony said. 'October thirty-first. November fifth.'

Light dawned. 'Hallowe'en. Bonfire Night.'

'Exactly.' As he always did when he was in the grip of an idea, he paced, pausing by the dining table to scribble down the odd note. 'What's special about them, Carol?'

'Well, people celebrate them. They do particular things. They're traditional.'

Tony grinned, his hands waving in the air as he spoke. 'Traditional. Exactly. That's it. You've hit the nail on the head. They're Great British traditions.'

'Hallowe'en's American,' Carol objected. 'Trick or treat. That's not British.'

'It is originally. It came from the Celtic Samhain festival. Trick or treat is a variation of the Scottish guising tradition. Trust me, Carol, it only got to be American when the Irish took it over there. We started it.'

Carol groaned. 'Sometimes I feel the internet is a terrible curse.'

'Not to those of us with inquiring minds. So, we've got two very British festivals. I can't help wondering if that's the root of what's going on here. Tina died like a witch on the ducking stool. Jonathan burned like a bonfire guy. The murder methods fit the dates.' He spun on his heel and headed back towards Carol.

'So I'm asking myself, is our killer somebody who's raging against Britain and our traditions? Someone who feels slighted by this country? Someone who feels racially oppressed, maybe? Because the victims are white, Carol. And the killer's paid no attention to Diwali. OK, we've not had Eid yet, but I'm betting he won't take a victim then. I'm telling you, Carol, I think I'm on to something here.'

Carol frowned. 'Even if you're right – and frankly, it sounds even more crazy than most of your theories – why these two? Why pick on them?'

Tony trailed to a halt and stared down at what he'd written. 'I don't know yet.' He turned to meet her eyes. 'But there is one thing I'm pretty sure about.'

He could see the dread in her eyes. 'What's that?'

'If we don't find the killer, the next victim's going to be a dead Santa. Stuffed in a chimney would be my best guess.'

Later, Tony's words would echo in Carol's head. When she least expected it, they reverberated inside her. As she sat in the canteen, half her attention on her lasagne and half on the screen of the TV, she was jolted by a newsflash that chilled her more than the November snow: SANTA SNATCHED OFF STREET.

II

It had been a long time since Tony had been a student, but he'd never lost his taste for research. What made his investigations different from those of Carol and her team was his conviction that the truth lay in the tangents. An exhaustive police investigation would turn up all sorts of unexpectedness, but there would always be stuff that slipped between the cracks. People were superstitious about telling secrets. Even when they gave up information, they held something back. Partly because they could and partly because they liked the illusion of power it dealt them. Tony, a man whose gift for empathy was his finest tool and his greatest weakness, had a remarkable talent for convincing people that their hearts would never be at peace till they had shared every last morsel of information.

And so he devoted his energies to identifying the unswept corners of the lives of Tina Chapman and Jonathan Meadows.

The first thing that attracted his attention about Tina Chapman was that she had only been in her current job for four years. In his world, history cast a long shadow, with present crimes often having their roots deep in the past. He wondered where Tina Chapman had been before she came to teach French in Leeds.

He knew he could probably short-circuit his curiosity with a call to Carol, but her jibe about the internet was still fresh in his mind so he decided to see what he could uncover without her help.

Googling Tina Chapman brought nothing relevant except for a Facebook entry describing her as 'everybody's favourite language teacher', an online review of the sixth form performance of *Le Malade Imaginaire* that she'd directed and a slew of news stories about the murder. None of the articles mentioned where she'd taught previously. But there was an interesting clue in one of them. Tina's son wasn't called Ben

Chapman but Ben Wallace. 'Lovely,' Tony said aloud. If Wallace had been Ben's father's name, there was at least a fighting chance that his mother had used it at some point.

He tried 'Tina Wallace' in the search engine, which threw out a couple of academics and a real estate agent in Wyoming. Then he tried 'Martina Chapman', 'Christina Chapman', 'Martina Wallace' and finally, 'Christina Wallace.' He stared at the screen, hardly able to credit what he saw there.

There was no doubt about it. If ever there was a motive for murder, this was it.

Detective Inspector Mike Cassidy knew Carol Jordan only by reputation. Her major case squad was despised and desired in pretty much equal measure by Bradfield's detectives, depending on whether they knew they would never be good enough or they aspired to join. Cassidy avoided either camp; at forty-two, he knew he was too old to find a niche working alongside the Chief Constable's blue-eyed girl. But he didn't resent her success as so many others did. That didn't stop him showing his surprise when she walked into his incident room with an air of confident ownership.

He stood up and rounded his desk, determined not to be put at a disadvantage. 'DCI Jordan,' he said with a formal little nod. He waited; let her come to him.

Carol returned the nod. 'DI Cassidy. I hear you're dealing with the abduction in Market Street?'

Cassidy's lips twisted in an awkward cross between a smile and a sneer. 'The case of the stolen Santa? Isn't that what they're calling it in the canteen?'

'I don't care what they're calling it in the canteen. As far as I'm concerned, there's nothing funny about a man being kidnapped in broad daylight on a Bradfield street.'

Cassidy took the rebuke on the chin. 'As it happens, I'm with you on that one, ma'am. It's no joke for Tommy Garrity or his family. And apart from anything else, it makes us look like monkeys.'

'So where are you up to?'

'Tommy Garrity was dressed in a Santa suit, collecting money for Christmas For Children when two men in balaclavas and blue overalls drove up the pedestrian precinct in a white Transit. They stopped in front of Tommy, bundled him into the Transit and took off. We got the van on CCTV, turns out it was stolen off a building site this morning.' Cassidy turned to his desk and excavated a map from the stack of paper by the keyboard. He handed it to Carol. 'The red line's the route they took out of the city centre. We lost them round the back of Temple Fields. Once you come off Campion Way, the coverage is patchy.'

Carol sighed. 'Typical. What about the number plate recognition cameras?'

'Nothing. At least we know they've not left the city on any of the main drags.'

'So, Tommy Garrity. Is he known?'

Cassidy shook his head. 'Nothing on file. He works

behind the bar at the Irish Club in Harriestown, does a lot of charity work in his spare time. He's fifty-five, three kids, two grandkids. Wife's a school dinner lady. I've got a team out on the knocker, but so far Garrity's white as the driven.'

Carol traced the line on the map. 'That's what worries me.'

Cassidy couldn't keep his curiosity at bay any longer. 'If you don't mind me asking, ma'am, what's your interest? I mean, not to play down the importance of daylight abduction, but it's not major in the sense of being up your street.'

Carol dropped the map on Cassidy's desk. 'Just something somebody said to me a couple of weeks ago. Can you keep me posted, please?'

Cassidy watched her walk out. She was more than easy on the eye, and normally that would have been all that registered with him. But Carol Jordan's inter-est had left him perturbed and anxious. What the hell was he missing here?

News generally passed Tony by. He had enough variety in his life to occupy his interest without having to seek out further examples of human shortcomings. But because he'd floated the suggestion of Santa as poten-tial victim, he was more susceptible than normal to the scream of newspaper billboards that announced, SANTA SNATCH IN CITY CENTRE.

The story in the paper was short on fact and long on frenzy, queasily uncertain whether it should be outraged or amused. Tony, already on his way to Carol's office, quickened his step.

He found her at her desk, reading witness statements from the Santa kidnap. She looked up and squeezed out a tired smile. 'Looks like you were right.'

'No, I wasn't. I mean, I think I was, but this isn't him.' Tony threw his hands in the air, exasperated at his inability to express himself clearly. 'This isn't the next victim in a series,' he said.

'What do you mean? Why not? You were the one who told me I should be looking out for Santa. And not in the sense of hanging up my stocking.'

'There were two of them. I never said anything about two of them.'

'I know you didn't. But it would have made the first two murders a lot easier if they'd been two-handed. And we both know that racially motivated fanatics tend to work in cells or teams. After what you said, I've had my crew looking at all our intel and we're not getting many hits on lone activists.' She shrugged. 'It may not have been in the profile but two makes sense.'

Tony threw himself in the chair. 'That's because I was ignoring my own cardinal rule. First you look at the victim. That's what it's all about, and I got distracted because of the eccentricity of the crimes. But I've looked at the victims now and I know why they were killed.' He fished some printouts from his carrier bag. 'Tina Chapman used to be known by her married name. She was Christina Wallace.' He passed the top sheet to Carol. 'She taught French at a school in Devon. She took a bunch of kids on a school trip and two of them drowned in a canoeing accident. The inquest cleared her, but the bereaved parents spoke to the press, blaming her for what happened. And it does look like they had pretty strong reasons for that. So, she moved away. Reverted to her maiden name and started afresh.'

'You think one of the parents did this?'

'No, no, that's not it. But once I knew that about Tina, I knew what I was looking for with Jonathan.' He handed over the second sheet. 'Seven years ago, a five-year-old girl was killed by a hit-and-run driver. The car was a Porsche that had allegedly been stolen from a garage where it was in for a service. The garage where Jonathan Meadows worked. I went over there and spoke to the local traffic officers. They told me that there was a strong feeling at the time that the Porsche hadn't been stolen at all, that Jonathan had taken it for a ride and had lost control. His DNA was all over the car but his excuse was that he'd been working on it. His girl-friend gave him an alibi and nothing ever came of it.'

Carol stared at the two sheets of paper. 'You're saying this is some kind of vigilante justice?'

Tony dipped his head. 'Kind of. Both victims were implicated in the death of a child but went unpunished because of legal loopholes or lack of evidence. The killer feels they stole children away from their fam-ilies. I think we should be looking for someone who has lost a child and believes nobody paid the price. Probably in the past year. He's choosing these victims because he believes they're culpable and he's choosing these murder methods because they mark the points in the year where parents celebrate with children.'

Within the hour, Tony and Carol were studying a list of seven children who had died in circumstances where blame might possibly be assigned. 'How can we narrow it down?' she demanded, frustration in her voice. 'We can't put surveillance on all these parents and their immediate families.'

'There's no obvious way,' Tony said slowly.

'Santa Garrity could still be a potential victim,' Carol said. 'We don't know enough about his history and there's nothing in your theory to say it couldn't be two killers working together.'

Tony shook his head. 'It's emotionally wrong. This is about punishment and pain, not justice. It's too personal to be a team effort.' He ran a hand through his hair. 'Couldn't we at least go and talk to the parents? Shake the tree?'

'It's a waste of time. Even you can't pick out a killer just by looking at them.' They sat in glum silence for a few minutes, then Carol spoke again. 'Victims. You're right. It all comes back to victims. How's he choosing his victims? You had to do some digging to come up with what you found. There was nothing in the public domain to identify Jonathan, and Tina had changed her name. That's why the motive didn't jump out at my team.'

Tony nodded. 'You're right. So who knows this

kind of information? It's not the police, there's at least two forces involved here. Not the Crown Prosecution Service either, neither of them ever got that far.'

Light dawned behind Carol's eyes. 'A journalist would know. They get access to all kinds of stuff. He could have recognised Tina Chapman from the press photographs at the time. If he has local police contacts, he could have heard that Jonathan Meadows was under suspicion over the hit and run.'

Tony scanned the list. 'Are any of these journalists?'

DI Cassidy entered the Children For Christmas offices almost at a run, his team at his heels. A trim little woman got to her feet and pointed to her computer screen. 'There. Just as it came in.'

The email was short but not sweet. 'We've got Santa. You've got money. We want £20,000 in cash. You'll hear from us in an hour. No police.'

'I thought I would ignore the bit about "no police",' the woman said. 'It's not as if we're going to be paying the ransom.'

Cassidy admired her forthrightness but had to check she was taking all the possibilities into consideration. 'You're not frightened they might kill Mr Garrity? Or seriously harm him?'

She gave him a scornful look. 'They're not going to hurt Santa. How do you think that would go down in prison? You of all people should know how sentimental criminals are.'

*

Carol's conviction that David Sanders was a serial killer took her no closer to making an arrest. There was a small matter of a complete lack of evidence against Sanders, a feature writer on the *Bradfield Evening Sentinel Times*. Even the apparent miracles of twenty-first-century forensic science couldn't nail this. Water and fire were notorious destroyers of trace evidence. She'd hoped that close analysis might fit together the cut marks on the tape and wire from the previous killings, but the fire had done too much damage. That meant there was no chance of definitively linking them to any materials still in Sanders' possession.

There were no reliable witnesses or meaningful CCTV footage. A couple of homeless men had turned up claiming to have seen Tina Chapman go into the canal. But the person pushing her had been wearing a Hallowe'en mask and the sighting had gone nowhere.

The only option left was to cling to Tony's conviction that the killer would strike again before Christmas. It was always hard to persuade her bosses to mount surveillance operations because they were so costly and because they took so many officers off other cases, but at least this one had a fixed end point.

And so they watched. They watched David Sanders go to work. They watched him drink in the pub with his workmates. They watched him work out at the gym. They watched him do his Christmas shopping. What they didn't watch him do was abduct and murder anyone.

Then it was Christmas Eve, the last day of authorised

surveillance. In spite of the privileges of rank, Carol put herself down for a shift. It was already dark when she slid into the passenger seat of the anonymous car alongside DC Paula McIntyre. 'Nothing moving, chief. He got home about an hour ago, nobody in or out since.'

'The house doesn't look very festive, does it? No sign of a tree or any lights.'

Paula, who had known her own share of grief, shrugged. 'You lose your only child? I don't expect Christmas is much to celebrate.'

The Sanders' four-year-old daughter had drowned during a swimming lesson back in September. The instructor had been dealing with another kid who was having a come-apart when Sanders' daughter had hit her head on the poolside. By the time anyone noticed, it had been too late. According to a colleague discreetly questioned by Sergeant Devine, it had ripped Sanders apart, though he'd refused to consider any kind of medical intervention.

Before Carol could respond, the garage door opened and Sanders' SUV crawled down the drive. They let him make it to the end of the street before they pulled out of their parking place and slipped in behind him. It wasn't hard to stay on the tail of the tall vehicle and fifteen minutes' driving brought them to a street of run-down terraced houses on the downtrodden edge of Moorside. On the corner was a brightly lit shop, its windows plastered with ads for cheap alcohol. Sanders pulled up and walked into the shop carrying a sports holdall.

'I think this is it,' Carol breathed. 'Let's go, Paula.'

They sprinted down the street and tried the door of the shop. But something was jamming it. Carol took a couple of steps back then charged the door, slamming her shoulder into the wooden surround. Something popped and the door crashed open.

Sanders was standing behind the counter, a cricket bat in his hand, dismay on his face. 'Police, drop your weapon,' Carol roared as Paula scrambled to the far end of the counter.

'There's someone here, chief. Looks like he's unconscious,' Paula said.

The cricket bat fell to the ground with a clatter. Sanders sank to the floor, head in hands. 'This is all your fault,' he said. 'You never make the right people pay the price, do you?'

Carol collapsed into Tony's armchair and demanded a drink. 'He didn't even bother with a denial,' she said. 'Being arrested seemed almost to come as a relief.' She closed her eyes for a moment, memory summoning up Sanders' haggard face.

'It generally does when you're not dealing with a psychopath,' Tony said.

Carol sighed. 'And a very merry bloody Christmas to you too.'

'You stopped him killing again,' Tony said, handing her a glass of wine. 'That's not an insignificant achievement.'

'I suppose. Jahinder Singh's family can celebrate

the festive season knowing their father's safe from any further consequences from selling solvents to kids.' Before Carol could say more, her phone rang. 'What now?' she muttered. She listened attentively, a slow smile spreading from mouth to eyes. 'Thanks for letting me know,' she said, ending the call. 'That was Cassidy. Santa's home free. Two extremely inept kidnappers are banged up and nobody got hurt.'

Tony raised his glass, his smile matching hers. In their line of work, making the best of a bad job was second nature. This wasn't exactly a happy ending, but it was closer than they usually managed. He'd settle for that any day.

A WIFE IN
A MILLION

The woman strolled through the supermarket, choosing a few items for her basket. As she reached the display of sauces and pickles, a muscle in her jaw tightened. She looked around, willing herself to appear casual. No one watched. Swiftly she took a jar of tomato pickle from her large leather handbag and placed it on the shelf. She moved on to the frozen meat section.

A few minutes later, she passed down the same aisle and paused. She repeated the exercise, this time adding two more jars to the shelf. As she walked on to the checkout, she felt tension slide from her body, leaving her light-headed.

She stood in the queue, anonymous among the morning shoppers, another neat woman in a well-cut winter coat, a faint smile on her face and a strangely unfocused look in her pale blue eyes.

Sarah Graham was sprawled on the sofa reading the Situations Vacant in the *Burnalder Evening News* when she heard the car pull up the drive. Sighing, she dropped the paper and went through to the kitchen. By the time she had pulled the cork from a bottle of elderflower wine and poured two glasses, the front door had opened and closed. Sarah stood, glasses in hand, facing the kitchen door.

Detective Sergeant Maggie Staniforth came into the kitchen, took the proffered glass and kissed Sarah perfunctorily. She walked into the living room and slumped in a chair, calling over her shoulder, 'And what kind of day have you had?'

Sarah followed her through and shrugged. 'Another shitty day in paradise. You don't want to hear my catalogue of boredom.'

'You never bore me. And besides, it does me good to be reminded that there's a life outside crime.'

'I got up about nine, by which time you'd probably arrested half a dozen villains. I whizzed through the *Guardian* job ads, and went down the library to check out the other papers. After lunch I cleaned the bedroom, did a bit of ironing and polished the dining-room furniture. Then down to the newsagent's for the evening paper. A thrill a minute. And you? Solved the crime of the century?'

Maggie winced. 'Nothing so exciting. Bit of breaking and entering, bit of paperwork on the rape case at the blues club. It's due in court next week.'

'At least you get paid for it.'

'Something will come up soon, love.'

'And meanwhile I go on being your kept woman.'

Maggie said nothing. There was nothing to say. The two of them had been together since they fell head over heels in love at university eleven years before. Things had been fine while they were both concentrating on climbing their career ladders. But Sarah's career in personnel management had hit a brick wall when the company that employed her had collapsed nine months previously. That crisis had opened a wound in their relationship that was rapidly festering. Now Maggie was often afraid to speak for fear of provoking another bitter exchange. She drank her wine in silence.

'No titbits to amuse me, then?' Sarah demanded. 'No funny little tales from the underbelly?'

'One that might interest you,' Maggie said tentatively. 'Notice a story in the *News* last night about a woman taken to the General with suspected food poisoning?'

'I saw it. I read every inch of that paper. It fills an hour.'

'Well, she's died. The news came in just as I was leaving. And there have apparently been another two families affected. The funny thing is that there doesn't seem to be a common source. Jim Bryant from casualty was telling me about it.'

Sarah pulled a face. 'Sure you can face my spaghetti carbonara tonight?'

The telephone cut across Maggie's smile. She quickly crossed the room and picked it up on the third ring. 'DS Staniforth speaking ... Hi, Bill.' She listened intently. 'Good God!' she exclaimed. 'I'll be with you in ten minutes. OK?' She stood holding the phone. 'Sarah ... that woman we were just talking about. It wasn't food poisoning. It was a massive dose of arsenic and two of the other so-called food poisoning cases have died. They suspect arsenic there too. I've got to go and meet Bill at the hospital.'

'You'd better get a move on, then. Shall I save you some food?'

'No point. And don't wait up, I'll be late.' Maggie crossed to Sarah and gave her a brief hug. She hurried out of the room. Seconds later, the front door slammed.

The fluorescent strips made the kitchen look bright but cold. The woman opened one of the fitted cupboards and took a jar of greyish-white powder from the very back of the shelf.

She picked up a filleting knife whose edge was honed to a wicked sharpness. She slid it delicately under the flap of a cardboard pack of blancmange powder. She did the same to five other packets. Then she carefully opened the inner paper envelopes. Into each she mixed a tablespoonful of the powder from the jar.

Under the light, the grey strands in her auburn hair glinted. Painstakingly, she folded the inner packets closed again and with a drop of glue she resealed the cardboard packages. She put them all in a shopping bag and carried it into the rear porch.

She replaced the jar in the cupboard and went through to the living room where the television blared. She looked strangely triumphant.

It was after three when Maggie Staniforth closed the front door behind her. As she hung up her sheepskin, she noticed lines of strain round her eyes in the hall mirror. Sarah appeared in the kitchen doorway. 'I know you're probably too tired to feel hungry, but I've made some soup if you want it,' she said.

'You shouldn't have stayed up. It's late.'

'I've got nothing else to do. After all, there's plenty of opportunity for me to catch up on my sleep.'

Please God, not now, thought Maggie. As if the job isn't hard enough without coming home to hassles from Sarah.

But she was proved wrong. Sarah smiled and said, 'So do you want some grub?'

'That depends.'

'On what?'

'Whether there's Higham's Continental Tomato Pickle in it.'

Sarah looked bewildered. Maggie went on. 'It seems that three people have died from arsenic administered in Higham's Continental Tomato Pickle bought from Fastfare Supermarket.'

'You're joking!'

'Wish I was.' Maggie went through to the kitchen. She poured herself a glass of orange juice as Sarah served up a steaming bowl of lentil soup with a pile of buttered brown bread. Maggie sat down and tucked in, giving her lover a disjointed summary as she ate.

'Victim number one: May Scott, fifty-seven, widow, lived up Warburton Road. Numbers two and three: Gary Andrews, fifteen, and his brother Kevin, thirteen, from Priory Farm Estate. Their father is seriously ill. So are two others now, Thomas and Louise Foster of Bryony Grange. No connection between them except that they all ate pickle from jars bought on the same day at Fastfare.

'Could be someone playing at extortion – you know, pay me a million pounds or I'll do it again. Could be someone with a grudge against Fastfare. Ditto against Higham's. So you can bet your sweet life we're going to be hammered into the ground on this one. Already we're getting flak.'

Maggie finished her meal. Her head dropped into her hands. 'What a bitch of a job.'

'Better than no job at all.'

'Is it?'

'You should know better than to ask.'

Maggie sighed. 'Take me to bed, Sarah. Let me forget about the battlefield for a few hours, eh?'

Piped music lulled the shoppers at Pinkerton's Hypermarket into a drugged acquisitiveness. The woman pushing the trolley was deaf to its bland presence and its blandishments. When she reached the shelf with the instant desserts on display, she stopped and checked that the coast was clear.

She swiftly put three packs of blancmange on the shelf with their fellows and moved away. A few minutes later she returned and studied several cake mixes as she waited for the aisle to clear. Then she completed her mission and finished her shopping in a leisurely fashion.

At the checkout she chatted brightly to the bored teenager who rang up her purchases automatically. Then she left, gently humming the song that flowed from the shop's speakers.

Three days later, Maggie Staniforth burst into her living room in the middle of the afternoon to find Sarah typing a job application. 'Red alert, love,' she announced. 'I'm only home to have a quick bath and change my things. Any chance of a sandwich?'

'I was beginning to wonder if you still lived here,' Sarah muttered darkly. 'If you were having an affair, at least I'd know how to fight back.'

'Not now, love, please.'

'Do you want something hot? Soup? Omelette?'

'Soup, please. And a toasted cheese sandwich?'

'Coming up. What's the panic this time?'

Maggie's eyes clouded. 'Our homicidal maniac has struck again. Eight people on the critical list at the General. This time the arsenic was in Garratt's Blancmange from Pinkerton's Hypermarket. Bill's doing a television appeal right now asking for people to bring in any packets bought there this week.'

'Different manufacturer, different supermarket. Sounds like a crazy rather than a grudge, doesn't it?'

'And that makes the next strike impossible to predict. Anyway, I'm going for that bath now. I'll be down again in fifteen minutes.' Maggie stopped in the kitchen doorway, 'I'm not being funny, Sarah. Don't do any shopping in the supermarkets. Butchers, greengrocers, OK. But no self-service, pre-packaged food. Please.'

Sarah nodded. She had never seen Maggie afraid in eight years in the force, and the sight did nothing to lift her depressed spirits.

This time it was jars of mincemeat. Even the Salvation Army band playing carols outside the Nationwide Stores failed to make the woman pause in her mission. Her shopping bag held six jars laced with deadly white powder when she entered the supermarket.

When she left, there were none. She dropped 50p in the collecting tin as she passed the band because they were playing her favourite carol, 'In the Bleak Midwinter'. She walked slowly back to the car park, not pausing to look at the shop-window Christmas displays. She wasn't anticipating a merry Christmas.

*

Sarah walked back from the newsagent's with the evening paper, reading the front page as she went. The Burnalder Poisoner was front-page news everywhere by now, but the stories in the local paper seemed to carry an extra edge of fear. They were thorough in their coverage, tracing any possible commercial connection between the three giant food companies that produced the contaminated food. They also speculated on the possible reasons for the week-long gaps between outbreaks. They laid out in stark detail the drastic effect the poisoning was having on the finances of the food-processing companies. And they noted the paradox of public hysteria about the poisoning while people still filled their shopping trollies in anticipation of the festive season.

The latest killer was Univex mincemeat. Sarah shivered as she read of the latest three deaths, bringing the toll to twelve. As she turned the corner, she saw Maggie's car in the drive and increased her pace. A grim idea had taken root in her brain as she read the long report.

While she was hanging up her jacket, Maggie called from the kitchen. Sarah walked slowly through to find her tucking into a plate of eggs and bacon, but without her usual large dollop of tomato ketchup. There were dark circles beneath her eyes and the skin around them was grey and stretched. She had not slept at home for two nights. The job had never made such demands on her before. Sarah found a moment to wonder if the atmosphere between them was partly responsible for Maggie's total commitment to this desperate search.

'How's it going?' she asked anxiously.

'It's not,' said Maggie. 'Virtually nothing to go on. No link that we can find. It's not as if we even have proper leads to chase up. I came home for a break because we were just sitting staring at each other, wondering what to do next. Short of searching everyone who goes into the supermarkets, what can we do? And those bloody reporters seem to have taken up residence in the station. We're being leaned on from all sides. We've got to crack this soon or we'll be crucified.'

Sarah sat down. 'I've been giving this some thought. The grudge theory has broken down because you can't find a link between the companies, am I right?'

'Yes.'

'Have you thought about the effect unemployment has on crime?'

'Burglary, shoplifting, mugging, vandalism, drugs, yes. But surely not mass poisoning, love.'

'There's so much bitterness there, Maggie. So much hatred, I've often felt like murdering those incompetent tossers who destroyed Liddell's and threw me on the scrapheap. Did you think about people who've been given the boot?'

'We did think about it. But only a handful of people have worked for all three companies. None of them have any reason to hold a grudge. And none of them have any connection with Burnalder.'

'There's another aspect, though, Maggie. It only hit me when I read the paper tonight. The *News* has a big piece about the parent companies who make the three products. Now, I'd swear that each one of those companies has advertised in the last couple of months for management executives. I know, I applied for two of the jobs. I didn't even get interviewed because I've got no experience in the food industry, only in plastics. There must be other people in the same boat, maybe less stable than I am.'

'My God!' Maggie breathed. She pushed her plate away. The colour had returned to her cheeks and she seemed to have found fresh energy. She got up and hugged Sarah fiercely. 'You've given us the first positive lead in this whole bloody case. You're a genius!'

'I hope you'll remember that when they give you your inspector's job.'

Maggie grinned on her way out the door. 'I owe you one. I'll see you later.'

As the front door slammed, Sarah said ironically, 'I hope it's not too late already, babe.'

Detective Inspector Bill Nicholson had worked with Maggie Staniforth for two years. His initial distrust of her gender had been broken down by her sheer grasp of the job. Now he was wont to describe her as 'a bloody good copper in spite of being a woman', as if this were a discovery uniquely his, and a direct product of working for him. As she unfolded Sarah's suggestion, backed by photostats of newspaper advertisements culled from the local paper's files, he realised for the first time she was probably going to leapfrog him on the career ladder before too long. He didn't like the idea, but he wasn't prepared to let that stand between him and a job of work.

They started on the long haul of speaking directly to the personnel officers of the three companies. It meant quartering the country and they knew they were working against the clock. Back in Burnalder, a team of detectives was phoning companies who had advertised similar vacancies, asking for lists of applicants. The lumbering machinery of the law was in gear.

On the evening of the second day, an exhausted Maggie arrived home. Six hundred and thirty-seven miles of driving had taken their toll and she looked crumpled and older by ten years. Sarah helped her out of her coat and poured her a stiff drink in silence.

'You were right,' Maggie sighed. 'We've got the name and address of a man who has been rejected by all three firms after the first interview. We're moving in on him tonight. If he sticks to his pattern, he'll be aiming to strike again tomorrow. So with luck, it'll be a red-handed job.' She sounded grim and distant. 'What a bloody waste. Twelve lives because he can't get a bloody job.'

'I can understand it,' Sarah said abruptly and went through to the kitchen.

Maggie stared after her, shocked but comprehending. She felt again the low rumble of anger inside her against a system that set her to catch the people it had so often made its victims. If only Sarah had not lost her well-paid job, then Maggie knew she would have left the force by now, but they needed her salary to keep their heads above water. The job itself was dirty enough; but the added pain of keeping her relationship with Sarah constantly under wraps was gradually becoming more than she could comfortably bear. Sarah wasn't the only one whose choices had been drastically pruned by her unemployment.

By nine fifty-five a dozen detectives were stationed around a neat detached house in a quiet suburban street. In the garden a 'For Sale' sign sprouted among the rose bushes. Lights burned in the kitchen and living room.

In the car, Bill made a final check of the search warrant. Then, after a last word over the radio, he and Maggie walked up the short drive.

'It's up to you now,' he said and rang the doorbell. It was answered by a tall, bluff man in his mid-forties. There were lines of strain round his eyes and his clothes hung loosely, as if he had recently lost weight.

'Yes?' he asked in a pleasant, gentle voice.

'Mr Derek Millfield?' Maggie demanded.

'That's me. How can I help you?'

'We're police officers, Mr Millfield. We'd like to have a word with you, if you don't mind.'

He looked puzzled. 'By all means. But I don't see what ...' His voice tailed off. 'You'd better come in, I suppose.'

They entered the house and Millfield showed them into a surprisingly large living room. It was tastefully and expensively furnished. A woman sat watching television.

'My wife Shula,' he explained. 'Shula, these are policemen – I mean officers. Sorry, miss.'

Shula Millfield stood up and faced them. 'You've come for me, then,' she said.

It was hard to say who looked most surprised. Then suddenly she was laughing, crying and screaming, all at once.

*

Maggie stretched out on the sofa. 'It was appalling. She must have been living on a knife-edge for weeks before she finally flipped. He's been out of work for seven months. They've had to take their kids out of private school, had to sell a car, sell their possessions. He had no idea what she was up to. I've never seen anyone go berserk like that. All for the sake of a nice middle-class lifestyle.

'There's no doubt about her guilt, either. Her fingerprints are all over the jar of arsenic. She stole the jar a month ago. She worked part-time in the pharmacy at the cottage hospital in Kincaple. But they didn't notice the loss. God knows how. Deputy heads will roll,' she added bitterly.

'What will happen to her?' Sarah asked coolly.

'She'll be tried, if she's fit to plead. But I doubt if she will be. I'm afraid it'll be the locked ward for life.' When she looked up, Maggie saw there were tears on Sarah's cheeks. She immediately got up and put an arm round her. 'Hey, don't cry, love. Please.'

'I can't help it, Maggie. You see, I know how she feels. I know that utter lack of all hope. I know that hatred, that sense of frustration and futility. There's nothing you can do to take that away. What you have to live with, Detective Sergeant Staniforth, is that it could have been me.

'It could so easily have been me.'

A
TRADITIONAL
CHRISTMAS

Last night, I dreamed I went to Amberley. Snow had fallen, deep and crisp and even, garlanding the trees like tinsel sparkling in the sunlight as we swept through the tall iron gates and up the drive. Diana was driving, her gloved hands assured on the wheel in spite of the hazards of an imperfectly cleared surface. We rounded the coppice, and there was the house, perfect as a photograph, the sun seeming to breathe life into the golden Cotswold stone. Amberley House, one of the little jobs Vanbrugh knocked off once he'd learned the trade with Blenheim Palace.

Diana stopped in front of the portico and blared the horn. She turned to me, eyes twinkling, smile bewitching as ever. 'Christmas begins here,' she said. As if on cue, the front door opened and Edmund stood framed in the doorway, flanked by his and Diana's mother, and his wife Jane, all smiling as gaily as daytrippers.

I woke then, rigid with shock, pop-eyed in the dark. It was one of those dreams so vivid that when you wake, you can't quite believe it has just happened. But I knew it was a dream. A nightmare, rather. For Edmund, sixth Baron Amberley of Anglezarke, had been dead for three months. I should know. I found the body.

Beside me, Diana was still asleep. I wanted to burrow into her side, seeking comfort from the horrors of memory, but I couldn't bring myself to be so selfish. A proper night's sleep was still a luxury for her and the next couple of weeks weren't exactly going to be restful. I slipped out of bed and went through to the kitchen to make a cup of camomile tea.

I huddled over the gas fire and forced myself to think back to Christmas. It was the fourth year that Diana and I had made the trip back to her ancestral home to celebrate. As our first Christmas together had approached, I'd worried about what we were going to do. In relationships like ours, there isn't a standard formula. The only thing I was sure about was that I wanted us to spend it together. I knew that meant visiting my parents was out. As long as they never have to confront the physical evidence of my lesbianism, they can handle it. Bringing any woman home to their tenement flat in Glasgow for Christmas would be uncomfortable. Bringing the daughter of a baron would be impossible.

When I'd nervously broached the subject, Diana had looked astonished, her eyebrows raised, her mouth twitching in a half-smile. 'I assumed you'd want to come to Amberley with me,' she said. 'They're expecting you to.'

'Are you sure?'

Diana grabbed me in a bearhug. 'Of course I'm sure. Don't you want to spend Christmas with me?'

'Stupid question,' I grunted. 'I thought maybe we

could celebrate on our own, just the two of us. Romantic, intimate, that sort of thing.'

Diana looked uncertain. 'Can't we be romantic at Amberley? I can't imagine Christmas anywhere else. It's so ... traditional. So English.'

My turn for the raised eyebrows. 'Sure I'll fit in?'

'You know my mother thinks the world of you. She insists on you coming. She's fanatical about tradition, especially Christmas. You'll love it,' she promised.

And I did. Unlikely as it is, this Scottish working-class lesbian feminist homeopath fell head over heels for the whole English country-house package. I loved driving down with Diana on Christmas Eve, leaving the motorway traffic behind, slipping through narrow lanes with their tall hedgerows, driving through the chocolate-box village of Amberley, fairy lights strung round the green, and, finally, cruising past the Dower House where her mother lived and on up the drive. I loved the sherry and mince pies with the neighbours, even the ones who wanted to regale me with their ailments. I loved the elaborate Christmas Eve meal Diana's mother cooked. I loved the brisk walk through the woods to the village church for the midnight service. I loved most of all the way they simply absorbed me into their ritual without distance.

Christmas Day was champagne breakfast, stockings crammed with childish toys and expensive goodies from the Sloane Ranger shops, church again, then presents proper. The gargantuan feast of Christmas dinner, with free-range turkey from the estate's home farm.

Then a dozen close family and friends arrived to pull crackers, wear silly hats and masks, drink like tomorrow was another life and play every ridiculous party game from Sardines to Charades. I'm glad no one's ever videotaped the evening and threatened to send a copy to the women's alternative health co-operative where I practise. I'd have to pay the blackmail. Diana and I lead a classless life in London, where almost no one knows her background. It's not that she's embarrassed. It's just that she knows from bitter experience how many barriers it builds for her. But at Amberley, we left behind my homeopathy and her Legal Aid practice, and for a few days we lived in a time warp that Charles Dickens would have revelled in.

On Boxing Day night, we always trooped down to the village hall for the dance. It was then that Edmund came into his own. His huntin', shootin' and fishin' persona slipped from him like the masks we'd worn the night before when he picked up his alto sax and stepped onto the stage to lead the twelve-piece Amber Band. Most of his fellow members were professional session musicians, but the drummer doubled as a labourer on Amberley Farm and the keyboard player was the village postman. I'm no connoisseur, but I reckoned the Amber Band was one of the best live outfits I've ever heard. They played everything from Duke Ellington to Glenn Miller, including Miles Davis and John Coltrane pieces, all arranged by Edmund. And of course, they played some of Edmund's own compositions, strange haunting slow-dancing pieces that somehow achieved the seemingly impossible marriage between the English countryside and jazz.

There was nothing different to mark out last Christmas as a watershed gig. Edmund led the band with his usual verve. Diana and I danced with each other half the night and took it in turns to dance with her mother the rest of the time. Evangeline ('call me Evie') still danced with a vivacity and flair that made me understand why Diana's father had fallen for her. As usual, Jane sat stolidly nursing a gin and tonic that she made last the whole night. 'I don't dance,' she'd said stiffly to me when I'd asked her up on my first visit. It was a rebuff that brooked no argument. Later, I asked Diana if Jane had knocked me back because I was a dyke.

Diana roared with laughter. 'Good God, no,' she spluttered. 'Jane doesn't even dance with Edmund. She's tone deaf and has no sense of rhythm.'

'Bit of a handicap, being married to Edmund,' I said.

Diana shrugged. 'It would be if music were the only thing he did. But the Amber Band only does a few gigs a year. The rest of the time he's running the estate and Jane loves being the country squire's wife.'

In the intervening years, that was the only thing that had changed. Word of mouth had increased the demand for the Amber Band's services. By last Christmas, the band were playing at least one gig a week. They'd moved up from playing village halls and hunt balls onto the student-union circuit.

Last Christmas I'd gone for a walk with Diana's mother on the afternoon of Christmas Eve. As we'd emerged from the back door, I noticed a three-ton van parked over by the stables. Along the side, in tall letters of gold and black, it said, 'Amber Band! Bringing jazz to the people'.

'Wow,' I said. 'That looks serious.'

Evie laughed. 'It keeps Edmund happy. His father was obsessed with breaking the British record for the largest salmon, which, believe me, was a far more inconvenient interest than Edmund's. All Jane has to put up with is a lack of Edmund's company two or three nights a week at most. Going alone to a dinner party is a far lighter cross to bear than being dragged off to fishing lodges in the middle of nowhere to be bitten to death by midges.'

'Doesn't he find it hard, trying to run the estate as well?' I asked idly as we struck out across the park towards the coppice.

Evie's lips pursed momentarily, but her voice betrayed no irritation. 'He's taken a man on part-time to take care of the day-to-day business. Edmund keeps his hands firmly on the reins, but Lewis has taken on the burden of much of the routine work.'

'It can't be easy, making an estate like this pay nowadays.'

Evie smiled. 'Edmund's very good at it. He understands the importance of tradition, but he's not afraid to try new things. I'm very lucky with my children, Jo. They've turned out better than any mother could have hoped.'

I accepted the implied compliment in silence.

*

The happy family idyll crashed around everyone's ears the day after Boxing Day. Edmund had seemed quieter than usual over lunch, but I put that down to the hangover that, if there were any justice in the world, he should be suffering. As Evie poured out the coffee, he cleared his throat and said abruptly, 'I've got something to say to you all.'

Diana and I exchanged questioning looks. I noticed Jane's face freeze, her fingers clutching the handle of her coffee cup. Evie finished what she was doing and sat down. 'We're all listening, Edmund,' she said gently.

'As you're all aware, Amber Band has become increasingly successful. A few weeks ago, I was approached by a representative of a major record company. They would like us to sign a deal with them to make some recordings. They would also like to help us move our touring venues up a gear or two. I've discussed this with the band, and we're all agreed that we would be crazy to turn our backs on this opportunity.' Edmund paused and looked around apprehensively.

'Congratulations, bro,' Diana said. I could hear the nervousness in her voice, though I wasn't sure why she was so apprehensive. I sat silent, waiting for the other shoe to drop.

'Go on,' Evie said in a voice so unemotional it sent a chill to my heart.

'Obviously, this is something that has implications for Amberley. I can't have a career as a musician and continue to be responsible for all of this. Also, we need to increase the income from the estate in order to make sure that whatever happens to my career, there will always be enough money available to allow Ma to carry on as she has always done. So I have made the decision to hand over the running of the house and the estate to a management company who will run the house as a residential conference centre and manage the land in broad accordance with the principles I've already established,' Edmund said in a rush.

Jane's face flushed dark red. 'How dare you?' she hissed. 'You can't turn this place into some bloody talking shop. The house will be full of ghastly sales reps. Our lives won't be our own.'

Edmund looked down at the table. 'We won't be here,' he said softly. 'It makes more sense if we move out. I thought we could take a house in London.' He looked up beseechingly at Jane, a look so naked it was embarrassing to witness it.

'This is extraordinary,' Evie said, finding her voice at last. 'Hundreds of years of tradition, and you want to smash it to pieces to indulge some hobby?'

Edmund took a deep breath. 'Ma, it's not a hobby. It's the only time I feel properly alive. Look, this is not a matter for discussion. I've made my mind up. The house and the estate are mine absolutely to do with as I see fit, and these are my plans. There's no point in argument. The papers are all drawn up and I'm going to town tomorrow to sign them. The other chaps from the village have already handed in their notice. We're all set.'

Jane stood up. 'You bastard,' she yelled. 'You inconsiderate bastard! Why didn't you discuss this with me?'

Edmund raised his hands out to her. 'I knew you'd be opposed to it. And you know how hard I find it to say no to you. Jane, I need to do this. It'll be fine, I promise you. We'll find somewhere lovely to live in London, near your friends.'

Wordlessly, Jane picked up her coffee cup and hurled it at Edmund. It caught him in the middle of the forehead. He barely flinched as the hot liquid poured down his face, turning his sweater brown. 'You insensitive pig,' she said in a low voice. 'Hadn't you noticed I haven't had a period for two months? I'm pregnant, Edmund, you utter bastard. I'm two months pregnant and you want to turn my life upside down?' Then she ran from the room slamming the heavy door behind her, no mean feat in itself.

In the stunned silence that followed Jane's bombshell, no one moved. Then Edmund, his face seeming to disintegrate, pushed his chair back with a screech and hurried wordlessly after his wife. I turned to look at Diana. The sight of her stricken face was like a blow to the chest. I barely registered Evie sighing, 'How sharper than a serpent's tooth,' before she too left the room. Before the door closed behind her, I was out of my chair, Diana pressed close to me.

Dinner that evening was the first meal I'd eaten at Amberley in an atmosphere of strain. Hardly a word was spoken, and I suspect I wasn't alone in feeling relief when Edmund rose abruptly before coffee and announced he was going down to the village to rehearse. 'Don't wait up,' he said tersely.

Jane went upstairs as soon as the meal was over. Evie sat down with us to watch a film, but half an hour into it, she rose and said, 'I'm sorry. I'm not concentrating. Your brother has given me rather too much to think about. I'm going back to the Dower House.'

Diana and I walked to the door with her mother. We stood under the portico, watching the dark figure against the snow. The air was heavy, the sky lowering. 'Feels like a storm brewing,' Diana remarked. 'Even the weather's cross with Edmund.'

We watched the rest of the film then decided to go up to bed. As we walked through the hall, I went to switch off the lights on the Christmas tree. 'Leave them,' Diana said. 'Edmund will turn them off when he comes in. It's tradition – last to bed does the tree.' She smiled reminiscently. 'The number of times I've come back from parties in the early hours and seen the tree shining down the drive.'

About an hour later, the storm broke. We were reading in bed when a clap of thunder as loud as a bomb blast crashed over the house. Then a rattle of machine-gun fire against the window. We clutched each other in surprise, though heaven knows we've never needed an excuse. Diana slipped out of bed and pulled back one of the heavy damask curtains so we could watch the hail pelt the window and the bolts of lightning flash jagged across the sky. It raged for nearly half an hour. Diana and I played the game of counting the gap between thunderclaps and lightning flashes, which told us the storm seemed to be circling Amberley itself, moving off only to come back and blast us again with lightning and hail.

Eventually it moved off to the west, occasional flashes lighting up the distant hills. Somehow, it seemed the right time to make love. As we lay together afterwards, revelling in the luxury of satiated sensuality, the lights suddenly went out. 'Damn,' Diana drawled. 'Bloody storm's got the electrics on the blink.' She stirred. 'I'd better go down and check the fuse box.'

I grabbed her. 'Leave it,' I urged. 'Edmund can do it when he comes in. We're all warm and sleepy. Besides, I might get lonely.'

Diana chuckled and snuggled back into my arms. Moments later, the lights came back on again. 'See?' I said. 'No need. Probably a problem at the local substation because of the weather.'

I woke up just after seven the following morning, full of the joys of spring. We were due to go back to London after lunch, so I decided to sneak out for an early morning walk in the copse. I dressed without waking Diana and slipped out of the silent house.

The path from the house to the copse was well-trodden. There had been no fresh snow since Christmas Eve, and the path was well used, since it was a short cut both to the Dower House and the village. There were even mountain-bike tracks among the scattered boot prints. The trees, an elderly mixture of beech, birch, alder, oak and ash, still held their tracery of snow on the tops of some branches, though following the storm a mild thaw had set in. As I moved into the wood, I felt drips of melting snow on my head.

In the middle of the copse, there's a clearing fringed with silver birch trees. When she was little, Diana was convinced this was the place where the fairies came to recharge their magic. There was no magic in the clearing that morning. As soon as I emerged from the trees, I saw Edmund's body, sprawled under a single silver birch tree by the path on the far side.

For a moment, I was frozen with shock. Then I rushed forward and crouched down beside him. I didn't need to feel for a pulse. He was clearly long dead, his right hand blackened and burned.

I can't remember the next hours. Apparently, I went to the Dower House and roused Evie. I blurted out what I'd seen and she called the police. I have a vague recollection of her staggering slightly as I broke the news, but I was in shock and I have no recollection of what she said. Diana arrived soon afterwards. When her mother told her what had happened, she stared numbly at me for a moment, then tears poured down her face. None of us seemed eager to be the one to break the news to Jane. Eventually, as if by mutual consent, we waited until the police arrived. We merited two uniformed constables, plus two plain-clothes detectives. In the words of Noël Coward, Detective Inspector Maggie Staniforth would not have fooled a drunken child of two and a half. As soon as Evie introduced me as her daughter's partner, DI Staniforth thawed visibly. I didn't much care at that point. I was too numbed even to take in what they were saying. It sounded like the distant mutter of bees in a herb garden.

DI Staniforth set off with her team to examine the body while Diana and I, after a muttered discussion in the corner, informed Evie that we would go and tell Jane. We found her in the kitchen drinking a mug of coffee. 'I don't suppose you've seen my husband,' she said in tones of utter contempt when we walked in. 'He didn't have the courage to come home last night.'

Diana sat down next to Jane and flashed me a look of panic. I stepped forward. 'I'm sorry, Jane, but there's been an accident.' In moments of crisis, why is it we always reach for the nearest cliché?

Jane looked at me as if I were speaking Swahili. 'An accident?' she asked in a macabre echo of Dame Edith Evans's 'A handbag?'

'Edmund's dead,' Diana blurted out. 'He was struck by lightning in the wood. Coming home from the village.'

As she spoke, a wave of nausea surged through me. I thought I was going to faint. I grabbed the edge of the table. Diana's words robbed the muscles in my legs of their strength and I lurched into the nearest chair. Up until that point, I'd been too dazed with shock to realise the conclusion everyone but me had come to.

Jane looked blankly at Diana. 'I'm so sorry,' Diana said, the tears starting again, flowing down her cheeks.

'I'm not,' Jane said. 'He can't stop my child growing up in Amberley now.'

Diana turned white. 'You bitch,' she said wonderingly. At least I knew then what I had to do.

Maggie Staniforth arrived shortly after to interview me. 'It's just a formality,' she said. 'It's obvious what happened. He was walking home in the storm and was struck by lightning as he passed under the birch tree.'

I took a deep breath. 'I'm afraid not,' I said. 'Edmund was murdered.'

Her eyebrows rose. 'You're still in shock. I'm afraid there are no suspicious circumstances.'

'Maybe not to you. But I know different.'

Credit where it's due, she heard me out. But the sceptical look never left her eyes. 'That's all very well,' she said eventually. 'But if what you're saying is true, there's no way of proving it.'

I shrugged. 'Why don't you look for fingerprints? Either in the plug of the Christmas tree lights, or on the main fuse box. When he was electrocuted, the lights fused. At the time, Diana and I thought it was a glitch in the mains supply, but we know better now. Jane would have had to rewire the plug and the socket to cover her tracks. And she must have gone down to the cellar to repair the fuse or turn the circuit breaker back on. She wouldn't have had occasion to touch those in the usual run of things. I doubt she'd even have good reason to know where the fuse box is. Try it,' I urged.

And that's how Evie came to be charged with the murder of her son. If I'd thought things through, if I'd waited till my brain was out of shock, I'd have realised that Jane would never have risked her baby by hauling Edmund's body over the crossbar of his mountain bike and wheeling him out to the copse. Besides, she probably believed she could use his love for her to persuade him to change his mind. Evie didn't have that hope to cling to.

If I'd realised it was Diana's mother who killed Edmund, I doubt very much if I'd have shared my esoteric knowledge with DI Staniforth. It's a funny business, New Age medicine. When I attended a seminar on the healing powers of plants given by a Native American medicine man, I never thought his wisdom would help me prove a murder.

Maybe Evie will get lucky. Maybe she'll get a jury reluctant to convict in a case that rests on the inexplicable fact that lightning never strikes birch trees.

THE LONG
BLACK VEIL

Jess turned fourteen today. With every passing year, she looks more like her mother. And it pierces me to the heart. When I stopped by her room this evening, I asked if her birthday awakened memories of her mother. She shook her head, leaning forward so her long blonde hair curtained her face, cutting us off from each other. 'Ruth, you're the one I think of when people say "mother" to me,' she mumbled.

She couldn't have known that her words opened an even deeper wound inside me and I was careful to keep my heart's response hidden from my face. Even after ten years, I've never stopped being careful. 'She was a good woman, your mother,' I managed to say without my voice shaking.

Jess raised her head to meet my eyes then swiftly dropped it again, taking refuge behind the hair. 'She killed my father,' she said mutinously. 'Where exactly does "good" come into it?'

I want to tell her the truth. There's part of me thinks she's old enough now to know. But then the sensible part of me kicks in. There are worse things to be in small-town America than the daughter of a murderess. So I hold my tongue and settle for silence.

Seems like I've been settling for silence all my adult life.

It's easy to point to where things end, but it's a lot harder to be sure where they start. Everybody here in Marriott knows where and when Kenny Sheldon died, and most of them think they know why. They reckon they know exactly where his journey to the grave started.

They're wrong, of course. But I'm not going to be the one to set them right. As far as Marriott is concerned, Kenny's first step on the road to hell started when he began dating Billy Jean Ferguson. Rich boys mixing with poor girls is pretty much a conventional road to ruin in these parts.

Me and Billy Jean, we were still in high school, but Kenny had a job. Not just any old job, but one that came slathered with a certain glamour. Somehow, he'd persuaded the local radio station to take him on staff. He was only a gofer, but Kenny being Kenny, he managed to parlay that into being a crucial element in the station's existence. In his eyes, he was on the fast track to being a star. But while he was waiting for that big break, Kenny was content to play the small-town big shot.

He'd always had an eye for Billy Jean, but she'd fended him off in the past. We'd neither of us been that keen on dating. Other girls in our grade had been hanging out with boyfriends for a couple of years by then, but to me and Billy Jean it had felt like a straitjacket. It was one of the things that made it possible for us to be best friends. We preferred to hang out at Helmer's drugstore in a group of like-minded teens, among them Billy Jean's distant cousin Jeff.

Their mothers were cousins, and by some strange quirk of genetics, they'd turned out looking like two peas in a pod. Hair the colour of butter, eyes the same shade as the hyacinths our mothers would force for Christmas. The same small, hawk-curved nose and cupid's bow lips. You could take their features one by one and see the correspondence. The funny thing was that you would never have mistaken Billy Jean for a boy or Jeff for a girl. Maybe it was nothing more than their haircuts. Billy Jean's hair was the long blonde swatch that I see now in Jess, whereas Jeff favoured a crew-cut. Still does, for that matter, though the blond is starting to silver round the temples now.

Anyhow, as time slipped by, the group we hung with thinned out into couples and sometimes there were just the three of us drinking Cokes and picking at cold fries. Kenny, who had taken to drifting into Helmer's when we were there, picked his moment and started insinuating himself into our company. He'd park himself next to Jeff, stretching his legs to stake out the whole side of the table. If either of us girls wanted to go to the bathroom, we had to go through a whole rigmarole of getting Kenny to move his damn boots. He'd lay an arm across the back of the booth proprietorially, a Marlboro dangling from the other hand, and tell us all about his important life at the radio station.

One night, he turned up with free tickets for a Del Shannon concert fifty miles down the interstate. We were impressed. Marriott had never seen live rock and roll, unless you counted the open mike night at the Tavern in the Town. As far as we were concerned, only the truly cool had ever seen live bands. It took no persuading whatsoever for us to accompany Kenny to the show.

What we hadn't really bargained for was Kenny treating it like a double date right from the start when he installed Billy Jean up front next to him in the car and relegated me and Jeff to the back seat. He carried on as he started, draping his arm over her shoulders at every opportunity. But we all were fired up with the excitement of seeing a singer who had actually had a number one single, so we all went along with it. Truth to tell, it turned out to be just the nudge Jeff and I needed to slip from friendship into courting. We'd been heading that way, but I reckon we'd both been reluctant to take any step that might make Billy Jean feel shut out. If Billy Jean was happy to be seen as Kenny's girlfriend – and at first, it seemed that way, since she showed no sign of objecting to the arm-draping or the subsequent hand-holding – then we were freed up to follow our hearts.

That first double date was a night to remember. The buzz from the audience as we filed into the arena was beyond anything we small-town kids had ever experienced. I felt like a little kid again, but in a good way. I slid my hand into Jeff's for security and we followed

Kenny and Billy Jean to our seats right at the front. When the support act took to the stage, I was rapt. Around us, people seemed to be paying no attention to the unknown quartet on the stage, but I was determined to miss nothing.

After Del Shannon's set, my ears were ringing from the music and the applause, my eyes dazzled by the spotlights glinting on the chrome and polish of the instruments. The air was thick with smoke and sweat and stale perfume. I was stunned by it all. I scarcely felt my feet touch the ground as we walked back to Kenny's car, the chorus of 'Runaway' ringing inside my head. But I was still alert enough to see that Kenny still had his arm round Billy Jean and she was leaning into him. I wasn't crazy about Kenny, but I was selfish. I wanted to be with Jeff so I wasn't going to try to talk Billy Jean out of him.

Kenny dropped Jeff and me off outside my house and as his tail lights disappeared, I said, 'You think she'll be OK?'

Jeff grinned. 'I've got a feeling Kenny just bit off more than he can chew. Billy Jean will be fine. Now, come here, missy, I've got something for you.' Then he pulled me into his arms and kissed me. I didn't give Billy Jean another thought that night.

Next day when we met up, we compared notes. I was still floating from Jeff's kisses and I didn't really grasp that Billy Jean was less enamoured of Kenny's attempts to push her well beyond a goodnight kiss. What I did take in was that she appeared genuinely pleased for Jeff and me. My fears that she'd feel shut out seemed to have been groundless, and she talked cheerfully about more double-dating. I didn't understand that was her way of keeping herself safe from Kenny's advances. I just thought that we were both contentedly coupled up after that one double date.

All that spring, we went out as a foursome. Kenny seemed to be able to get tickets to all sorts of venues and we went to a lot of gigs. Some were good, most were pretty terrible and none matched the excitement of that first live concert. I didn't really care. All that mattered to me was the shift from being Jeff's friend to being his girlfriend. I was in love, no doubting it, and in love as only a teenage girl can be. I walked through the world starry-eyed and oblivious to anything that wasn't directly connected to me and my guy.

That's why I paid no attention to the whispers linking Kenny's name to a couple of other girls. Someone said he'd been seen with Janine who tended bar at the Tavern in the Town. I dismissed that out of hand. According to local legend, a procession of men had graced Janine's trailer. Why would Kenny lower himself when he had someone as special as Billy Jean for a girlfriend? Oh yes, I was quite the little innocent back in the day.

Someone else claimed to have seen him with another girl at a blues night in the next county. I pointed out to her that he worked in the music business. It wasn't surprising if he had to meet with colleagues at music events. And that it shouldn't surprise her if some of those colleagues happened to be women. And that it was a sad day when women were so sexist.

I didn't say anything to Billy Jean, even though we were closer than sisters. I'd like to think it was because I didn't want to cause her pain, but the truth is that their stories probably slipped my mind, being much less important than my own emotional life.

By the time spring had slipped into summer, Jeff and I were lovers. I'm bound to say it was something of a disappointment. I suspect it is for a lot of women. Not that Jeff wasn't considerate or generous or gentle. He was all of those and more. But even after we'd been doing it a while and we'd had the chance to get better at it, I still had that Peggy Lee, 'Is that all there is?' feeling.

I suppose that made it easier for me to support Billy Jean in her continued refusal to let Kenny go all the way. When we were alone together, she was adamant that she didn't care for him nearly enough to let him be the one to take her virginity. For my part, I told her she should hold out for somebody who made her dizzy with desire because frankly that feeling was the only thing that made it all worth it.

The weekend after I said that to her, Billy Jean told Kenny she wasn't in love with him and she didn't want to go out with him any more. Of course, he went around telling anybody who would listen that he was the one to call time on their relationship, but I suspect that most people read that for the bluster it was. 'How did he take it?' I asked her at recess on the Monday afterwards. 'Was he upset?'

'Upset, like broken-hearted? No way.' Billy Jean gave a little 'I could give a shit' shrug. 'He was really pissed at me,' she said. 'I got the impression he's the only one who gets to decide when it's over.'

'You know, I've been wanting to say this for the longest time, but he really is kind of an asshole,' I said.

We both giggled, bumping our shoulders into each other like big kids. 'I only started going out with him so you and Jeff would finally get it together,' Billy Jean said in between giggles. 'I knew as long as I was single you two would be too loyal to do anything about it. Now I can just go back to having you both as my best friends again.'

And so it played out over the next few weeks. Billy Jean and I hung out together doing girl things; Billy Jean and Jeff went fishing out on the lake once a week and spent Sunday mornings fixing up the old clunker her dad had bought for her birthday; we'd all go for a pizza together on Friday nights; and the rest of the time she'd leave us to our own devices. It seemed like one chapter had closed and another had opened.

Jess turned fourteen today. Seems like yesterday she came into our home. It wasn't how we expected it to be, me and Ruthie. We thought we'd have a brood of our own, not end up raising my cousin's kid. But some things just aren't meant to be and I'm old enough now to know there are sometimes damn good reasons for that.

I remember the morning after Jess was conceived. When Billy Jean told Ruthie and me what Kenny Sheldon had done,

I didn't think it was possible to feel more angry and betrayed. I was wrong about that too, but that's another story.

It happened the night before, when Ruthie and I were parked up by the lake in my car and Billy Jean was on her lonesome, nursing a Coke in one of the booths at Helmer's. According to her, when Kenny walked in, he didn't hesitate. He came straight over to her booth and plonked himself down opposite her. He gave her the full charm offensive, apologising for being mean to her when she'd thrown him over.

He claimed he'd missed her and he wanted her back but if he couldn't be her boyfriend he wanted to be her friend, like me. He pitched it just right for Billy Jean and she believed he meant what he said. That's the kind of girl she was back then – honest and open and unable to see that other people might not be worthy of her trust. So she didn't think twice when he offered her a ride home.

She called me first thing Sunday morning. We were supposed to be going fishing as usual but she wanted Ruthie to come along too. I could tell from her voice something terrible had happened even though she wouldn't tell me what it was, so I called Ruthie and got her to make some excuse to get out of church.

When we picked her up, she was pale and withdrawn. She wouldn't say a word till we were out at the lake, sitting on the jetty with rods on the water like it was any other Sunday morning. When she did speak, it was right to the point. Billy Jean was never one for beating about the bush, but this was bald, even for her.

'Kenny Sheldon raped me last night,' she said. She told us about the meeting at Helmer's and how she'd agreed to

let him drive her home. Only, before they got to her house, Kenny had driven down an overgrown track out of sight of the street. Then he'd pinned her down and forced her to have sex with him.

We didn't know what to do. Fourteen years ago, date rape wasn't on the criminal agenda. Not in towns like Marriott. And the Sheldons were a prominent family. Kenny's dad owned the funeral home and had been a councilman. And his mom ran the flower-arranging circle at the church. Whereas the Fergusons were barely one step up from white trash. Nobody was going to take the word of Billy Jean Ferguson against Kenny Sheldon.

I wanted to call Kenny Sheldon out and beat him to within an inch of his life. I wanted him to beg for mercy the way I knew Billy Jean had begged him the night before.

But Ruthie and Billy Jean stopped me. 'Don't stoop so low,' Billy Jean said.

'That's right,' Ruthie said. 'There's other ways to get back at scum like him.'

And by that afternoon, I had started the rumour that Janine from the Tavern in the Town had stopped sleeping with Kenny because she'd found out he had a venereal disease. I don't know how long it took to get back to the shitheel himself, but I do know he'd had quite the struggle to get anyone to sit next to him in Helmer's, never mind hang out at gigs with him. That cheered us up some, and Ruthie said Billy Jean was starting to talk about getting over it. That was so like her – she wasn't the kind to let anybody take her life away from her. She was always determined to control her own destiny.

But all her good intentions went to shit about six weeks after the rape. I'd been helping my dad finish off some work in the top pasture and both girls were sitting on the front porch when I got back to the house. We all piled into my truck and headed out to the lake. We hadn't gone but half a mile when Ruthie blurted out, 'She's pregnant. That bastard Kenny got her pregnant.'

I only had to glance at Billy Jean to know it was true and the knowledge made me boiling mad. I swung the truck round at the next intersection and headed for the Sheldon house, paying no mind to the girls shouting at me to stop. When we got there, I jumped out and marched straight up to the house. I hammered on the door and Kenny himself opened it.

I know that violence isn't supposed to solve things, but in my experience, it definitely has its plus points. I grabbed Kenny by the shirt front, yanked him out the door and slammed him against the wall. I swear the whole damn house shook. 'You bastard,' I yelled at him. 'First you rape her, then you get her pregnant.'

I drew my hand back to smack him in the middle of his dumbfounded face, but Billy Jean caught my arm. She was always strong for a girl and she had me at an awkward angle. 'Leave him,' she said. 'I don't want anything to do with him.'

'You say that now, but you're going to need his money,' I snarled. 'Babies don't come cheap and he has to pay for what he's done.'

Before anybody could say anything more, Mrs Sheldon appeared in the doorway. She looked shocked to see her golden boy pinned up against the wall and demanded to know what was going on.

My dander was up, and I wasn't about to back off. 'Ma'am,' I said, 'I'm sorry to cause a scene, but your son here raped my cousin Billy Jean and now she is expecting his baby.'

Mrs Sheldon reared back like a horse spooked by a snake. 'How dare you,' she hissed. 'My son is a gentleman, which is more than I can say about you or your kin.' She made a kind of snorting noise in the back of her throat. 'The very idea of any Ferguson woman being able to name the father of her children with any certainty is absurd. Now get off my property before I call the police. And take your slut of a cousin with you.'

It was my turn to grab Billy Jean. I thought she was fixing to rip Mrs Sheldon's face off. 'You evil witch,' she screamed as I pulled her away.

Ruthie stared Mrs Sheldon down. When she spoke, her voice was cold and sharp. I know I hoped she'd never use that tone of voice to me. 'You should be ashamed of yourself,' she said, turning on her heel and walking back to the truck, head high. I never knew to this day whether she meant Kenny or his mother or both of them.

What happened that evening must have had some effect, though. A week later, Kenny was gone.

Back in the early sixties, being an unwed mother was still about the biggest disgrace around and most girls who got into trouble ended up disowned and despised. But Billy Jean was lucky in her parents. The Fergusons never had much money but they had love aplenty. When she told them she was pregnant and how it had happened, they'd been shocked, but they hadn't been angry with her. Her father went round to see old man Sheldon. He never told anybody what passed between them, not even Mrs Ferguson, but he came back with a cashier's check for ten thousand dollars.

Nobody knew where Kenny was. His mother told her church crowd that he'd landed a big important radio job out on the coast, but nobody believed her. Truth to tell, I don't think anybody much cared. We certainly didn't.

Jeff and I were married three months later. I guess we were both kind of fired up by Billy Jean being pregnant. We wanted to start a family of our own. We moved into a little house on Jeff's daddy's farm and Jeff started working as a trainee sales representative for an agricultural machinery firm.

Half a mile down the track from us there was an old double-wide trailer that had seen better days. Jeff's dad used to rent it out to seasonal workers. We persuaded him to let Billy Jean have it for next to nothing in return for doing it up. We knew there wasn't enough room in her parents' house for Billy Jean and a growing kid, and I wanted her to be close at hand so we could bring up our children together.

Jeff and I spent most of our spare time knocking that trailer into shape. Billy Jean helped as much as she could, and by the time Jess was born, we'd turned it into a proper little home for the two of them. They moved in when Jess was six weeks old, and Billy Jean looked relaxed for the first time since Kenny had raped her. 'I can never thank the two of you enough,' she said so many times I told her she should just make a tape of it and give us each a copy.

'It was Ruthie's idea,' Jeff said, acting like it was nothing to do with him.

'I know,' Billy Jean said. 'But I also know you did more than your fair share to make it happen.'

We settled into a pretty easy routine. I worked mornings on the farm, helping Jeff's mother with the speciality yoghurt business she was building up. Afternoons, I'd hang out with Billy Jean and Jess. Then I'd cook dinner for Jeff, we'd either watch some TV or walk down to have a beer and a few hands of cards with Billy Jean. Most people might have thought our lives pretty dull, but it seemed fine enough to us.

There was one thing, I thought, that stopped it being perfect. A year had gone by since Jeff and I had married, but still I wasn't pregnant. It wasn't for want of trying, but I began to wonder whether my lack of enthusiasm for sex was somehow preventing it. I knew this was crazy, but it nagged away at me.

Finally, I managed to talk to Billy Jean about it. It was a hot summer afternoon and Jess was over at her grandma's house. Billy Jean and I were lying on her bed with the only a/c in the trailer cranked up high. 'I love him,' I said. 'But when we make love, it's not like it says in the books and magazines. It doesn't feel like it looks in the movies. I just don't feel that whole swept away thing.'

Billy Jean rolled over on to her back and yawned.

'I'm not the best person to ask, Ruth. I only ever had sex the once and that sure wasn't what you would call a good experience. I don't guess it's the kind of thing you can talk to Jeff about either.'

I made a face. 'He'd be mortified. He thinks I think he's the greatest lover on the planet.' Billy Jean giggled. 'Well, you have to make them feel like that.'

Billy Jean yawned again. 'I'm sorry, Ruth. I don't mean you to feel like I'm dismissing you, but I am so damn tired. I was up three times with Jess last night. She's teething.'

'Why don't you just have a nap?' I said. But she was already drifting away. I made myself more comfortable and before I knew it, I'd nodded off too.

I woke because someone was kissing me. An arm was heavy across my chest and shoulder, a leg was thrown between mine and soft lips were pressing on mine, a tongue flicking between my lips. I opened my eyes and the mouth pulled back from mine. A face that was familiar and yet completely strange hovered above mine. *Jeff with long hair*, I thought stupidly for a moment before the truth dawned.

Billy Jean put a finger to my lips. 'Ssh,' she said 'Let's see if we can figure out what Jeff's doing wrong.'

By the end of the afternoon, I understood that it wasn't what Jeff did that was wrong. It was who he was.

Kenny came back a couple of weeks before Jess's fourth birthday. It turned out his mother hadn't been lying to the church group. He had landed a job working for a radio station in

Los Angeles. He was doing pretty well. Had his own show and everything. He rolled back into town in a muscle car with a beautiful blonde on his arm. His fiancée, apparently.

All of that would have been just fine if he had left the past alone. But no. He wanted to impress the fiancée with his credentials as a family man. The first thing we knew about it was when Billy Jean got a letter from Kenny's lawyer saying he planned to file suit for shared custody. Kenny wanted Jess for one week a month until she started school, then he wanted her for half the school vacations. If he'd been the standard absent father as opposed to one who had never even seen his kid, it might have sounded reasonable. And we had a sneaking feeling that the court might see things Kenny's way.

Justice in Marriott comes courtesy of His Honour Judge Wellesley Benton. Who is an old buddy of Kenny Sheldon's daddy and a man who's put a fair few of Billy Jean's relatives behind bars. We were, to say the least, apprehensive.

The day after the letter came, Billy Jean happened to be walking down Main Street when Kenny strolled out of the Coffee Bean Scene with the future Mrs Sheldon. I heard all about it from Mom, who saw it all from the vantage point of the quilting store porch.

Billy Jean just lit into him. Called him all the names under the sun from rapist to deadbeat dad. Kenny looked shocked at first, then when he saw his fiancée wasn't turning a hair, he started to laugh. That just drove Billy Jean even crazier. She was practically hysterical. Mom came over from the quilt shop and grabbed her by the shoulders, trying to get her away. Then Kenny said, 'I'll see you in court,' and walked his fiancée to the car. Billy Jean was fit to be tied.

Well, everybody thinks they know what happened next. That night, Kenny was due at a dinner in the Town Hall. As he approached, a figure stepped out of the shadows. Long blonde hair, jeans and a Western shirt, just like Billy Jean always liked to wear. And a couple of witnesses who were a ways off but who knew Billy Jean well enough to recognise her when she raised the shotgun and blew Kenny Sheldon into the next world.

That was the end of her as much as it was the end of him.

I knew Billy Jean was innocent. Not out of some crazy misplaced belief, but because at the very moment Kenny Sheldon was meeting his maker, I was in her bed, moaning at her touch. That first afternoon had not been a one-off. It had been an awakening that had led us both into a deeper happiness than we'd ever known before.

If I'd been married to anyone other than Jeff, I'd have left in a New York minute. But I cared about him. More importantly, so did Billy Jean. 'You're both my best friend,' she said as we lay in a tangle of sheets. 'Until this afternoon, I couldn't have put one of you above the other. You gotta stay with him, Ruth. You gotta go on being his wife because I couldn't live with myself if you didn't.'

And so I did. It might seem strange to most folks, but in a funny kind of way, it worked out just fine for us. Except of course that I still couldn't get pregnant. I began to think of that as the price I had to pay for my other contentments – Jeff, Billy Jean, Jess.

Then Kenny came back.

They came for Billy Jean soon after midnight. A deputy we'd all been at school with knocked on our door at one in the morning, carrying Jess in a swaddle of bedclothes. He looked mortified as he explained what had happened and asked us to take care of the child till morning when things could be sorted out more formally.

Jess had often stayed with us, so she settled pretty easy. That morning, I drove into town, leaving Jess with her grandma, and demanded to see Billy Jean. She was white and drawn, her eyes heavy and haunted. 'They can't prove it,' she said. 'You have to promise me you will never tell. Don't sacrifice yourself trying to save me. They won't believe you anyway and you'll have shamed yourself in their eyes for nothing. Just have faith. We both know I'm innocent. Judge Benton isn't a fool. He won't let them away with it.'

And so I kept my mouth shut. Partly for Billy Jean and partly for Jess. We'd already made arrangements with Billy Jean and her parents for me and Jeff to take care of Jess till after the court case, and I wasn't about to do anything that would jeopardise that child's future. I sat through that terrible trial day after day. I listened to witnesses swearing they had seen Billy Jean kill Kenny Sheldon and I said not a word.

Nor did Billy Jean. She said she was somewhere else, but refused to say where or with whom. Judge Benton offered her the way out. 'Woman, what is your alibi?' he thundered. 'If you were somewhere else that night, then you won't have to die. If you're telling the truth, give up your alibi.' But she wouldn't budge. And so I couldn't. It nearly killed me.

But I never truly thought he would have her hanged.

I never truly thought he would have her hanged. I thought they'd argue she was temporarily insane because of the threat to her child and that she'd do a few years in jail, nothing more. And I was selfish enough to think of how much my Ruthie would love bringing up Jess for as long as Billy Jean was behind bars.

Sure, I wanted to make her suffer. But I didn't want her to die. She was my best friend, after all. A friend like no other. I swear, I always believed we would lay down our lives for each other if it came to it. And I guess I was right, in a way. She laid down her life rather than destroy my marriage.

When the sentence came down, it hit me like a physical blow. I swear I doubled over in pain as I realised the full horror of what I'd done. But it was too late. The sacrifices were made, the chips down once and for all.

I saw the way she looked at me in court. A mixture of pity and blame. As soon as she heard those witnesses, recognised the conviction in their voices, I think she knew the truth. With a long blonde wig and the right clothes, I could easily be mistaken for her.

There was an excuse for the witnesses. They were a way off from Kenny and his killer. But there's no excuse for Ruthie. She was no distance at all from Billy Jean that afternoon I saw them by the lakeshore. She could not have been mistaken.

Why didn't I confront her? Why didn't I walk away? I

guess because I loved them both so much. I didn't want to lose the life we had. I just wanted Billy Jean to suffer for a while, that was all. I never truly thought he would have her hanged.

Jess turned fourteen today. She's not old enough for the truth. Maybe she'll never be that old. But there's one thing she is old enough for.

Tonight, there will be two of us standing over Billy Jean's grave, our long black veils drifting in the wind, our tears sparkling like diamonds in the moonlight.

THE GIRL
WHO KILLED
SANTA CLAUS

It was the night before Christmas, and not surprisingly, Kelly Jane Davidson was wide awake. It wasn't that she wanted to be. It wasn't as if she believed in Santa and expected to catch him coming down the chimney onto the coal-effect gas fire in the living room. After all, she was nearly eight now.

She felt scornful as she thought back to last Christmas when she'd still been a baby, a mere six-year-old who still believed that there really was an elf factory in Lapland where they made the toys; that there really was a team of reindeer who magically pulled a sleigh across the skies and somehow got round all the world's children with sackloads of gifts; that she could really write a letter to Santa and he'd personally choose and deliver her presents.

Of course, she'd known for ages before then that the fat men in red suits and false beards who sat her on their knees in an assortment of gaudy grottoes weren't the real Santa. They were just men who dressed up and acted as messengers for the real Father Christmas, passing on her desires and giving her a token of what would be waiting for her on Christmas morning.

She'd had her suspicions about the rest of the story, so when Simon Sharp had told her in the playground that there wasn't really a Santa Claus, she hadn't even felt shocked or shaken. She hadn't tried to argue, not like her best friend Sarah who had gone red in the face and looked like she was going to burst into tears. But it was obvious when you thought about it. Her mum was always complaining when she ordered things from catalogues and they sent the wrong thing. If the catalogue people couldn't get a simple order right, how could one fat man and a bunch of elves get the right toys to all the children in the world on one night?

So Kelly Jane had said goodbye to Santa without a moment's regret. She might have been more worried if she hadn't discovered the secret of the airing cupboard. Her mum had been downstairs making the tea, and Kelly Jane had wanted a pillow case to make a sleeping bag for her favourite doll. She'd opened the airing cupboard and there, on the top shelf, she'd seen a stack of strangely shaped plastic bags. They were too high for her to reach, but she'd craned her neck and managed to see the corner of some packaging inside one of the bags. Her heart had started to pound with excitement, for she'd immediately recognised the familiar box that she'd been staring at in longing in the toyshop window for weeks.

She'd closed the door silently and crept back to her room. Her mum had said, 'Wait and see what Santa brings you,' as if she was still a silly baby, when she'd asked for the new Barbie doll. But here it was in the house.

Later, when her mum and dad were safely shut in the living room watching the telly, she'd crept out of bed and used the chair from her bedroom to climb up and explore further. It had left her feeling very satisfied. Santa or no Santa, she was going to have a great Christmas.

Which was why she couldn't sleep. The prospect of playing with her new toys, not to mention showing them off to Sarah, was too exciting to let her drift off into dreams. Restless, she got out of bed and pulled the curtains open. It was a cold, clear night, and in spite of the city lights, she could still see the stars twinkling and the thin crescent of the moon like a knife cut in the dark blue of the sky. No sleigh, or reindeers, though.

She had no idea how much time had passed when she heard the footsteps. Heavy, uneven thuds on the stairs. Not the light-footed tread of her mum, nor the measured footfalls of her dad. These were stumbling steps, irregular and clumsy, as if someone was negotiating unfamiliar territory.

Kelly Jane was suddenly aware how cold it had become. Her arms and legs turned to gooseflesh, the short hair on the back of her neck prickling with unease. Who – or what – was out there, in her house, in the middle of the night?

She heard a bump and a muffled voice grunting, as if in pain. It didn't sound like anyone she knew. It didn't even sound human. More like an animal. Or some sort of monster, like in the stories they'd read at school at Hallowe'en. Trolls that ate little children. She'd remembered the trolls, and for weeks she'd taken the long way home to avoid going over the ring-road flyover. She knew it wasn't a proper bridge like trolls lived under, but she didn't want to take any chances. Sarah had agreed with her, though Simon Sharp had laughed at the pair of them. It would have served him right to have a troll in his house on Christmas Eve. It wasn't fair that it had come to her house, Kelly Jane thought, trying to make herself angry to drive the fear away.

It didn't work. Her stomach hurt. She'd never been this scared, not even when she had to have a filling at the dentist. She wanted to hide in her wardrobe, but she knew it was silly to go somewhere she could be trapped so easily. Besides, she had to know the worst.

On tiptoe, she crossed the room, blinking back tears. Cautiously, she turned the door handle and inched the door open. The landing light was off, but she could just make out a bulky shape standing by the airing cupboard. As her eyes adjusted to the deeper darkness, she could see an arm stretching up to the top shelf. It clutched the packages and put them in a sack. Her packages! Her Christmas presents!

With terrible clarity, Kelly Jane realised that this was no monster. It was a burglar, pure and simple. A bad man had broken into her house and was stealing her Christmas presents! Outrage flooded through her, banishing fear in that instant. As the bulky figure put the last parcel in his sack and turned back to the stairs, she launched herself through the door and raced towards the landing, crashing into the burglar's legs just as he took the first step. 'Go away, you bad burglar,' she screamed.

Caught off balance, he crashed head over heels down the stairs, a yell of surprise splitting the silence of the night like an axe slicing through a log.

Kelly Jane cannoned into the bannisters and rebounded onto the top step, breathless and exhilarated. She'd stopped the burglar! She was a hero!

But where were her mum and dad? Surely they couldn't have slept through all of this?

She opened their bedroom door and saw to her dismay that their bed was empty, the curtains still wide open. Where were they? What was going on? And why hadn't anyone sounded the alarm?

Back on the landing, she peered down the stairs and saw a crumpled heap in the hallway. He wasn't moving. Nervously, she decided she'd better call the police herself.

She inched down the stairs, never taking her eyes off the burglar in case he suddenly jumped up and came after her.

Step by careful step, she edged closer.

Three stairs from the bottom, enough light spilled in through the glass panels in the front door for Kelly Jane to see what she'd really done.

There, in the middle of the hallway, lay the prone body of Santa Claus. Not moving. Not even breathing.

She'd killed Santa Claus.

Simon Sharp was wrong. Sarah was right. And now Kelly Jane had killed him.

With a stifled scream, she turned tail and raced back to her bedroom, slamming the door shut behind her. Now she was shivering in earnest, her whole body trembling from head to foot. She dived into bed, pulling the duvet over her head. But it made no difference. She felt as if her body had turned to stone, her blood to ice. She couldn't stop shaking, her teeth chattering like popcorn in a pan.

She'd killed Santa Claus.

All over the world, children would wake up to no Christmas presents because Kelly Jane Davidson had murdered Santa. And everyone would know whom to blame, because his dead body was lying in her hallway. Until the day she died, people would point at her in the street and go, 'There's Kelly Jane Davidson, the girl who murdered Christmas.'

Whimpering, she lay curled under her duvet, terrible remorse flooding her heart. She'd never sleep again.

But somehow, she did. When her mum threw open the door and shouted 'Merry Christmas!' Kelly Jane was sound asleep. For one wonderful moment, she forgot what had happened. Then it came pouring back in and she peered timidly over the edge of the duvet at her mum. She didn't seem upset or worried. How could she have missed the dead body in the hall?

'Don't you want your presents?' her mum asked. 'I can't believe you're still in bed. It's nine o'clock. You've never slept this late on Christmas morning before. Come on, Santa's been!'

Nobody knew that better than Kelly Jane. What had happened? Had the reindeer summoned the elves to take Santa's body away, leaving her presents behind? Was she going to be the only child who had Christmas presents this year? Reluctantly, she climbed out of bed and dawdled downstairs behind her mum, gazing in worried amazement at the empty expanse of the hall carpet.

She trailed into the living room, feet dragging with every step. There, under the tree, was the usual pile of brightly wrapped gifts. Kelly Jane looked up at her mum, an anxious frown on her face. 'Are these all for me?' she asked. Somehow, it felt wrong to be rewarded for killing Santa Claus.

Her mum grinned. 'All for you. Oh, and there was a note with them as well.' She handed Kelly Jane a Christmas card with a picture of reindeer on the front.

Kelly Jane took it gingerly and opened it. Inside in shaky capital letters, it read, DON'T WORRY. YOU CAN NEVER KILL ME. I'M MAGIC. HAPPY CHRISTMAS FROM SANTA CLAUS.

A slow smile spread across her face. It was all right! She hadn't murdered Santa after all!

Before she could say another word, the door to the kitchen opened and her dad walked in. He had the biggest black eye Kelly Jane had ever seen, even on the telly. The whole of one side of his face was all bruised, and his left arm was encased in plaster. 'What happened, Dad?' she asked, running to hug him in her dismay.

He winced. 'Careful, Kelly, I'm all bruised.'

'But what happened to you?' she demanded, stepping back.

'Your dad had a bit too much to drink at the office party last night,' her mum said hastily. 'He had a fall.'

'But I'm going to be just fine. Why don't you open your presents?' he said, gently pushing Kelly Jane towards the tree.

As she stripped the paper from the first of her presents, her mum and dad stood watching. 'That'll teach me to leave you alone in the house on Christmas Eve,' her mum said softly.

Her dad tried to smile, but gave up when the pain kicked in. 'Bloody Santa suit,' he said. 'How was I to know she'd take me for a burglar?'

HOLMES
FOR
CHRISTMAS

I n the ten years since Sherlock Holmes and I had last spent a night under the same roof, time had wrought many changes for both of us. My momentous decision to propose marriage to our landlady Mrs Hudson had provoked my old friend to send for the carriers and pack up the contents of his rooms in her house at 221B Baker Street. He had left London before the banns for our nuptials were called and disappeared from our lives overnight. I had no means of reaching him to invite him to our wedding breakfast for he had left no forwarding address.

His silence grieved me, for we had shared so many adventures over the years. I had foolishly thought our friendship meant as much to Holmes as it did to me. At first I felt as bereaved as I had been by the death of my late wife Mary. But Mrs Hudson – as I continued to call her, for I had become so accustomed to it – soon saw to it that my life was full and fascinating, and I admit that in a surprisingly short time, I had almost grown used to his absence.

Full five years passed before we were to meet again. I ventured out from Baker Street one morning in 1908 heading for my club, only to be knocked off my feet by a young man rushing past. He paused momentarily and shouted, 'The beggar by the National Gallery,' before continuing on his way.

Such an encounter would be entirely baffling to most men, but to one who had spent so many years at the side of the greatest consulting detective in the world, it seemed nothing less than a clarion call to action. I hastened up Baker Street to the tube station and descended to the Bakerloo Line, still a novelty in our district. A mere matter of minutes later, I emerged at Trafalgar Square, a short walk from the pillared edifice of the National Gallery. As I approached, I could see a huddled heap of rags shaking a tin cup at passers-by, wheedling for alms. He could not have looked less like Holmes, but I knew better than to be taken in by that.

I marched straight up to him and said, 'You sent for me, Holmes?'

A wizened toothless face looked up at me and cackled. ''E said you'd be 'ere.'

I swallowed my indignation at having been tricked yet again by my old friend. 'Who said?'

'Mr 'olmes – 'e said you were to give me an 'alf-crown to tell you where 'e is.'

I fished a coin from my purse, held it where the ruined man could see it, and said, 'It's yours when you tell me.'

He gestured upwards with his thumb and there, leaning against a pillar in the portico, stood Holmes, his narrow hawkish face as inscrutable as ever. I tossed the half-crown at the beggar and took the steps as quickly as I could manage with my cane. 'Holmes,' I exclaimed. 'It's good to see you, but what need had you of such a rigmarole? You are always welcome in Baker Street.'

A shadow passed across his face. 'Another day, perhaps. Today it would grieve me still further to visit my old haunts.'

'My old friend,' I said, concerned at his tone as much as his words. 'What grieves you so?'

He looked away and spoke, his voice curiously flat and toneless. 'I had word last night. Irene Adler is dead.'

I took an involuntary step backwards. 'Irene Adler, dead? Can you be certain, Holmes?'

'As certain as if I had seen her body myself. The report comes from a man in Geneva that I would trust with my own life. She was struck down by cholera and died within three days.' He cleared his throat. 'Walk with me, Watson?'

And so we set off down Whitehall to the river, where we walked for hours, pausing only when he observed my need to rest my leg. We had little need of words. I knew of Irene Adler's significance to Holmes. She was the one foe who had defeated him; he had referred to her ever afterwards as 'the woman'. Beneath the surface of the words was an emotional turbulence I had never found the courage to explore.

That meeting was the resurrection of our friendship. Thenceforward, Holmes would send me a telegram every two or three months, suggesting a meeting. Often we had dinner at my club, but sometimes we would pass a few hours walking through the city parks.

He would never return to Baker Street, however. Three years into this new phase of our relationship, Holmes invited me to his retirement cottage on the edge of the South Downs, where he had taken up beekeeping.

Thus one wintry morning in 1911 the train carried me through a landscape made ghostly with frost to Eastbourne station. I was met by a splendidly polished dark green Austin Landaulette, driven by Holmes' man Hogg, a taciturn Cumbrian in early middle age. I was still somewhat apprehensive of motor cars, but with Hogg I felt in safe hands in spite of the icy roads. We soon covered the three and a half miles to East Dean, where Holmes' substantial cottage sat on one side of the village green, opposite the ancient white-washed Tiger Inn.

Inside, the main room of the cottage bore a startling resemblance to our lodgings in Baker Street, except that where a series of bullet holes had once spelled out VR, a new set now read GR. We spent a pleasant time over a splendid lunch provided by Mrs Hogg, and Holmes held forth on the subject of his bees. Afterwards, he led the way to an extensive orchard at the rear of the house and we toured the hives as the day faded. He finished his account of the work of the queens and said abruptly, 'I should like it if you were to bring your wife when next you visit, Watson.'

'Mrs Hudson would be delighted,' I replied with alacrity. And indeed she was. Our visits became a regular quarterly outing and so it was that we found ourselves on Christmas Eve 1913, sitting round a blazing fire with tumblers of eggnog, looking out at the blizzard sweeping past the windows.

'I fear we must be snowed in,' my wife said cheerfully. 'Even your splendid Landaulette would make no headway in this. Nothing could be more fitting for Christmas.'

I knew that for Holmes, Christmas was no more special than any other day, but my friend had taken to making an effort to be more charming to my wife than he had ever managed when she was our landlady. 'And we are well provisioned,' he said. 'Mrs Hogg assures me we have supplies enough for a siege.'

Mrs Hogg had clearly also had a hand in the decoration of the room. A lavish swag of holly, mistletoe and Christmas roses adorned the fireplace and a pie-crust side table held a neat pyramid of small parcels wrapped in coloured paper decorated with pretty hand-painted motifs. My wife had given a wry smile on first entering the room; in our days in Baker Street, Holmes had always been contemptuous of such displays. I wondered whether he had indeed mellowed with age or if it was simply that he no longer cared for such small domestic battles.

Holmes stood up to add more wood to the crackling fire, and glanced out of the window, exclaiming softly. I followed his gaze and to my astonishment saw a figure labouring through the heavy flurries of snow. He was a big man, wrapped in a long plaid cloak, a bonnet on his head. He used a gnarled staff like a shepherd's crook to help keep his footing among the treacherous drifts. He appeared to be making for the venerable Tiger Inn on the far side of the green, but he stopped abruptly when he drew level with Holmes' cottage. He stared fixedly at the window against which Holmes must have been outlined, then turned away and continued his progress to the inn.

As he disappeared inside, Holmes gave me a quizzical look. 'What do you make of that, my old friend?'

'A late traveller arriving at the inn, startled by the light from your window?' I ventured.

'On Christmas Eve?' Holmes demanded crisply.

'He looked like a Scotchman to me,' my wife remarked.

'You have keen eyesight, Mrs Hudson,' our host observed. He turned back to the window. 'I suppose he will arrive at our door after breakfast.'

I had no idea how he arrived at such a conclusion, but the years had taught me to feel no surprise the following morning when Mrs Hogg entered the breakfast room to announce that Holmes had a visitor. We had already partaken of an excellent breakfast of apples cooked in honey followed by lamb chops with quail eggs and fried potatoes, so his arrival provided no inconvenience except to delay our exchange of Christmas gifts. 'Show him into the parlour,' Holmes said.' Watson and I will join him as soon as we have finished our coffee, if Mrs Hudson will excuse us?'

I sensed a moment's relief in my wife's smile. 'Indeed, Mr Holmes. Mrs Hogg has promised to show me her recipe for Sussex Pond Pudding.' Of course, she knew full well that I should relate whatever occurred when next we were alone. We may once have believed we had secrets from Mrs Hudson, but I know better now.

We entered the parlour to find our visitor standing by the window contemplating the swirling snow beyond. He turned as we entered and looked Holmes up and down, as if taking the measure of him for combat. He was a burly giant of a man, with a dense mop of startling ginger hair and a well-groomed beard to match. He had unfastened his cloak to reveal a tweed suit the colour of a grouse moor in August.

'Take a seat, Mr Stewart,' Holmes said pleasantly. 'Travelling from Appin at this time of year cannot have been an easy journey.'

Our visitor looked startled. 'How do you know my name? Or where I come from?' His Highland origins were obvious even in those few words.

Holmes chuckled and made his way to his favourite armchair. 'Your plaid is unmistakably the variant of the Royal Stewart tartan as worn by the Stewarts of Appin. Your Tam O'Shanter' – he gestured at the man's bonnet – 'carries the white cockade of those who supported the Jacobite rebellion of 1745 and its desire to see Bonnie Prince Charlie crowned King Charles III. And your staff is not the style of walking stick that any city dweller would carry.'

He gave a hearty laugh and threw himself into the chair opposite Holmes. 'Well done, sir. I am Alexander Stewart of the house of Appin, as you rightly said. And I believe you are the only man alive who can help me.'

Holmes steepled his long fingers and raised an eyebrow. 'I dare say you are correct. But I am retired. Unless you seek advice about apiculture, there is nothing I can do for you.'

Stewart seemed undaunted. 'Nevertheless, I cannot believe you will turn down the opportunity to restore the true king of Scotland to his throne.'

Stewart's story was a fantastical one, but Holmes listened with every sign of belief. The Highlandman reminded us that in May of that year, parliament had passed the Scottish Home Rule Bill, laying out provisions for a devolved administration responsible for much of Scotland's governance. But its provisions had failed to satisfy a growing desire north of the border for a complete severance from the rest of the United Kingdom.

'The movement is growing daily, Mr Holmes,' Stewart said earnestly. 'But what we need is a charismatic figure to rally round. And I believe I know of such a man. The true king of Scotland lives and breathes, sir.'

'Interesting. But why do you need my services?'

Stewart wrung his Tam O'Shanter in his hands. 'Because we don't know where he is.'

Holmes leaned forward. 'What makes you so certain such a person even exists? History tells us that Prince Charles Edward Stewart died without issue. His brother was a celibate priest, a Cardinal of the Church of Rome. There is no heir.' I never ceased to be amazed at the extent and detail of Holmes' knowledge.

Stewart's face lit up in a smile that creased his cheeks. 'That's what people have been led to believe. But we know differently. After Bonnie Prince Charlie set sail from France to raise the standard for the '45 rebellion, his brother Henry, Duke of York, followed him to France. The duke was received at the court of Louis XV at Versailles, then he went on to Dunkirk where he was supposed to raise money, ships and soldiers to support his brother's campaign once Charles had reached the south of England.

'Henry was stuck there for six weary months, struggling to raise an invading army. He was bored and lonely, and as men will when they are bored and lonely, he formed an attachment to a local girl. She became pregnant with his child and they entered into a secret marriage.' He sat back in his chair, taking a pipe and a pouch of tobacco from his pocket.

As he began to fill his pipe, Holmes stared at him. 'This is the same Cardinal York who was notorious in the Vatican for surrounding himself with beautiful young men?'

Stewart flushed. 'A vile rumour. The marriage and the child are facts, not scurrilous gossip.'

'How is it that this has never come to light?' Holmes began to fill his own pipe, a smile playing on his lips.

'The priest was ordered by his superiors to destroy the records. But some months ago, a young man from Dunkirk arrived in Appin with a family bible. We have no reason to doubt its authenticity.' He took a small oilskin satchel from a poacher's pocket in his plaid and unlatched it to reveal a leather-bound book which he held out to Holmes.

My friend held it with delicate fingers, sniffing it and scrutinising its binding. He reached for the magnifying glass on the table next to him and studied it more closely. Finally, he opened it and inspected the endpapers. Then he passed it to me. 'What do you make of it, Watson?'

The page showed a succession of entries, in different inks and different hands. It appeared to be a list of names. Individual names were followed by an 'n' or an 'm' – which I took to mean 'ne' or 'mort' – and a date. Two names connected by a + sign and an 'm' and a date I took to indicate marriage. The list began in 1723 and the most recent entry was dated just over a year ago. 'It looks like a typical family bible,' I said. 'It seems authentic to me.'

Holmes grunted and gestured for me to pass it back to him. He frowned at the spidery hands that crawled down the page. 'I take it these are the entries you are interested in?' He pointed to two lines. The first read, 'Catherine Petit + Henri LeDuc, m, 14 Oct 1745.' The second succinctly reported, 'Charles Henri LeDuc, n, 3 Avr 1746.'

Stewart nodded. 'The child was born shortly before Henry had to return to Paris after the tragic defeat at Culloden. Nobody knew where Prince Charles was, and it fell to Henry to raise funds to find him and rescue him. In his eyes, his duty to his brother and to Scotland was greater than his obligation to his wife and son. As far as we know, he never returned to Dunkirk, and then a year later he left Paris for Rome and the priesthood. But you can see from this bible that his legitimate son Charles grew up to marry and father a son and three daughters. The line continues unbroken until the birth of Henri LeDuc twenty years ago in 1893.'

Holmes nodded. 'But how is it that you cannot lay your hand on young Henri LeDuc? It seems none of his clan has ever strayed far from their native heath.'

'We have the story from the laddie who brought us the bible. He is Edouard LeDuc, the younger and only brother of Henri. You'll see his birth recorded two years after.' He leaned forward to point Holmes to a line in the bible. 'The LeDuc family are millers in Dunkirk. Henri worked for his father, who is, by Edouard's account, a violent and dictatorial man. Henri fell in love with a lassie who worked in a tavern and he was determined to marry her. When his father found out, he beat Henri to within an inch of his life and said he would finish the job unless his son gave up the girl. As soon as he had recovered, Henri stole his father's meagre savings and disappeared without a trace. All Edouard knows is that Henri was determined to travel as far as he could from his father, earn enough money to support himself and a family, then send for his love.'

'It's a pretty tale,' Holmes said. 'And common enough to be credible. But why have the LeDucs surfaced now? And what does young Edouard seek to gain?'

Stewart finished tamping his tobacco and lit his pipe, filling the room with the fragrance of peat and heather. 'According to Edouard, their right to the Scottish throne has always been a family legend. But with no throne to claim, no country to rule, it remained just that, a legend – until a few weeks ago, when a Scottish fishing boat put into the harbour at Dunkirk. The crew were drinking in one of the harbourside taverns and when the owner learned where they were from, he joked that they had come to the kingdom of the true ruler of their country. And the Scottish fishermen said that such a notion might not be a joke, if the Scots had their way. Parliament was offering them crumbs, but many of their countrymen thought it was time for the whole loaf. Nobody took them seriously. It was all drunken high spirits. But Henri's paramour was working in the tavern that night and she passed on to Edouard what the men had been saying.'

It was clear from Stewart's passionate telling of his tale that he believed every word. Holmes was more sceptical. 'And so Prince Edouard made his way to Appin to lay claim to the throne?'

'No!' Stewart's denial was vehement. 'Edouard wants nothing for himself. He made his way to the library of the Faculty of Advocates in Edinburgh, where he sought information about the royal house of Stuart. There, he learned that our branch of the clan is what some might call the keeper of the Jacobite flame. So he duly arrived on my doorstep with his bible and his story. And I am here now because I believe him and I think you are the one man in the world who can find King Henry the First of Scotland. And find him before his enemies do. For there are many who would think nothing of taking a life to preserve Westminster's rule over my country.'

'You're laying a great deal of weight on a family bible with no supporting documents,' Holmes said casually.

Stewart coloured. 'There is more.' From his oilskin pouch he drew something, keeping his hand closed. He opened his fingers to reveal a gold brooch in the shape of two entwined hearts surmounted by a crown. One heart was studded with diamonds, the other with rubies. 'It's a luckenbooth, a traditional Scottish design,' Stewart said. 'Edouard LeDuc says it's a family heirloom. That his father will kill him when he discovers it's missing.'

He handed it to Holmes, who scrutinised it minutely under his magnifying glass. 'A princely bauble indeed,' he said. Something caught his eye and he peered more closely. 'There is an engraving here.'

'Where?' Stewart looked startled.

'On the inside edge of this heart. It's tiny, almost invisible. "To MS from HS"'

Stewart's eyes widened. 'To Mary Stuart from Henry Stuart,' he breathed. 'A love token from Henry Stuart, Lord Darnley, to his wife, Mary Queen of Scots. A royal family heirloom passed down to Henry, Duke of York, from his great-great-grandmother. If proof you seek, Mr Holmes, there it is. Now, I beg you – find my king.'

*

'Stewart's story is all very well,' I said as our Christmas feast drew to a close, 'But he has provided you with not a single thread to follow. Even his brother has not a clue where Henri LeDuc is to be found. Should you take up his challenge.'

My wife chuckled. 'James, there is nothing Mr Holmes likes better than an impossible challenge.'

'Once that was true, dear lady. But these days I am a simple beekeeper.'

She shook her head, mock-woeful. 'Inhabiting the Valley of Fear? Sir, I never thought I would see the day, but I believe you have met your match.'

Something flashed in Holmes dark eyes. 'Were I to pursue this, madam, I can assure you it would present few challenges to my skills. But apparently I must repeat myself. I am no longer a consulting detective, I am a simple beekeeper.'

And so we left it. But barely two weeks later, I received a cryptic telegram from Holmes: 'The Scotsman, p13'. My curiosity piqued, I made my way to King's Cross station where I knew I could find a vendor selling the Scottish papers. I opened the *Scotsman* where I stood and there, tucked away towards the bottom of the page, was a small report.

A visiting Frenchman was killed yesterday evening in Edinburgh in an incident involving a motor car. M. Edouard LeDuc, a miller from Dunkirk in Northern France, died instantly when he was knocked down by a Morris Oxford

> Bullnose driven by an Edinburgh man. M. LeDuc
> was crossing Princes Street outside the North
> British Hotel near Waverley Steps when the acci-
> dent took place. Witnesses said the car appeared
> to accelerate towards M. LeDuc, but Edinburgh
> police said later that the Frenchman had walked
> out in front of the car without warning.

It appeared that Alexander Stewart had been telling the truth when he had spoken of enemies who would stop at nothing to prevent the Stuart line reclaiming their throne. Shocked, I walked home in a daze.

I showed the article to my wife, who was equally taken aback. 'That's the end of simple beekeeping,' she said shrewdly. 'Mark my words, James, he will already be miles away from East Dean.'

And so it proved. I sent Holmes a wire that very afternoon, but I had no reply. Months passed without a word until at last, in late May, another telegram arrived. 'To see the end of what you saw begun, join me in Trieste by 21 June; 14 Via Andrea Palladio will find me. Ask for the beekeeper.'

My wife uttered that sentence so beloved of spouses everywhere. 'I told you so. I knew the death of Edouard LeDuc would prove irresistible to him.'

'But why Trieste? It's in Italy, is it not? Not France? What is Henri LeDuc doing in Italy?'

'The question that is more to the point, James, is, will you go?'

A tiny smile twitched at the corner of her lips and I

knew at once I had her support in the inevitable decision that lay before me.

Via Andrea Palladio in Trieste did not live up to the reputation of its namesake, the great Renaissance architect. It was a narrow, deserted thoroughfare lined with undistinguished buildings whose stucco was in urgent need of repair and redecoration. The shutters in the upper storeys were firmly closed against the stifling heat of the day. It did not possess an atmosphere of welcome.

I lifted the weighty iron ring that served as a knocker on the heavy double doors bearing the number 14 and heard a hollow echo behind them. A minute at least passed before one side creaked open to reveal a muscular young man in tight trousers and a greasy singlet. 'I'm here to see the beekeeper,' I said, pretending to a confidence I did not feel.

He nodded. '*Aspetta, dottore,*' and closed the door.

My Italian was sufficient to know that I was being commanded to wait, and the addition of '*dottore*' made me a little less wary.

Before long, the young man returned and handed me a sealed envelope. '*A voi,*' he said with a slight bow, then closed the door again.

The envelope contained a card that simply said, '6 p.m. station café'. Holmes clearly believed I would answer his call. Presumably he would be at the station every evening at 6 p.m. until 21 June, a mere two days away.

I passed the intervening hours in a café near the port with a carafe of decent red wine and a strange sort of pie called lasagne, composed of layers of a stew of minced beef and tomatoes, a white sauce, and thin pasta topped with cheese. It was tasty enough, but its soft texture felt more like invalid food to me. I resolved to say nothing about it to my wife lest she consider adding it to her kitchen repertoire.

The magnificent frontage of the station lay beyond a wide piazza that bustled with people heading in every direction. I scanned the crowds as I crossed it but saw no sign of Holmes nor of any suspicious followers. The café was a small dark bolthole tucked away between the ticket booths and the platforms. It was busy with men drinking coffee, beer and small glasses of clear spirit. They crowded round the bar or stood at high circular tables, some engaged in lively conversation, others gazing morosely at their drinks. None of them resembled my friend, but it was hard to see every corner of the room. I pushed through to the bar and ordered a glass of beer. As it arrived, a voice at my shoulder said softly, 'You will not be sorry you came, Watson.'

I swung round and there was Holmes, resplendent in a cream linen suit and a panama hat set at a jaunty angle on his narrow head. He carried a silver-topped cane and looked every inch the Italian gentleman. 'Holmes!' I exclaimed, taking in his tanned features. 'You look well.'

'Let us go somewhere more private,' he proposed. I left my beer untasted and followed him out of the station and across the street to a grand hotel where Holmes was greeted with the respect and affection normally accorded to a well-respected regular patron. We took the lift to the second floor and Holmes led me to a spacious suite overlooking the station piazza.

I settled gratefully into an armchair that was more comfortable than it appeared and Holmes leaned against the mantelpiece. As he spoke, he filled and lit his pipe, the familiar aroma of his cheap black shag filling the room. I wondered that even on the far side of Europe he was still able to secure a ready supply of the working man's smoke. 'I know where he is,' he began.

'You mean – you've tracked down Henri LeDuc?'

Holmes nodded. 'I believe so. I have quartered the continent in these past months, following a trail that at times led me into blind alleys, at times petered out altogether and yet still reappeared when I thought all was lost. But I am sure of the latest information that has come to me. Henri LeDuc is working as a cashier in Schiller's Delicatessen in Sarajevo.'

'In Sarajevo?' I echoed. 'The Balkans.'

'Well done, Watson. It is presently part of the Austro-Hungarian Empire but the territories in the Balkans are like shifting sands.'

'What is LeDuc doing in Sarajevo?'

'He appears to be doing nothing more sinister than totting up bills and accepting customers' payments in a delicatessen.'

'But why there?'

Holmes shrugged. 'The Balkans are one of the poorest regions in Europe. The money he has earned on his wanderings will go further there. I suspect he wants to impress his bride-to-be with the appearance of prosperity. Perhaps a small farm, or a mill of his own?'

'So you have fulfilled the task set by Alexander Stewart,' I exclaimed.

'My task will not be complete until I hand the young king over to his clan. We must winkle him out of Sarajevo and bring him safely back to Scotland. And that, my dear Watson, will be more of a challenge that it at first appears.'

'How so?'

'You will remember Stewart spoke of being beset with enemies of the nationalist cause? The Unionists are desperate to take Henri LeDuc off the chessboard for good. Our paths have already crossed on this quest. And they might have succeeded had the man they had chosen as an assassin had the courage of his convictions.' Holmes spoke casually, as if assassination were as commonplace as kippers for breakfast.

'What happened?'

'As you know, they murdered his brother, but that was in Edinburgh. They clearly lack the necessary nerve to repeat the exercise on foreign soil. I was hot on LeDuc's trail a week ago here in Trieste. I caught sight of him one evening on the quayside but before I could approach, I spotted a young man making straight for him. A stray shaft of light glinted on a blade in his hand. I doubted I could reach him in time to save Le Duc. He raised his arm to strike but at the last minute, he turned away and fled.'

'Holmes!' I exclaimed. 'Did you not warn LeDuc?'

'I was more concerned with tracking his would-be assassin. I followed him to a disreputable tavern by the docks and kept watch. He drank several glasses of that disgusting spirit the Italians brew from grape stalks, then he approached a pair of men huddled together in a corner. They engaged in a lengthy conversation, and when my quarry left, he was in high spirits.'

'Where did he go?'

'Back to a small *pensione*. I returned to the tavern and made inquiries. The men he spoke to belong to a secret military society dedicated to unification of the southern Balkan states. They're called the Black Hand.'

'But why would a Scotch Unionist have dealings with a Balkan gang?'

'They need funds to organise and they are happy to earn them in any way they can. They have no qualms about assassination, Watson.'

'Then why are we wasting time here in Trieste when we should be protecting Henri LeDuc?' I sprang to my feet.

Holmes chuckled. 'Sit down, Watson. Do you think I have been idle? I am still a master of disguise and they are too arrogant to believe they can be spied upon. The Black Hand, in the pay of the Scottish Unionists, will move against LeDuc on June twenty-eighth.'

'Why are they waiting?'

Holmes exhaled a long trail of smoke. 'There will be a

diversion. Archduke Ferdinand is due to visit Sarajevo and the Black Hand have already made threats against his life that they intend to pursue that day. I gather that there will be a determined effort to assassinate the Archduke in the course of his tour of the city. All the attention of the police and the military will be focused on the Archduke and his entourage in the centre of the city. Nobody will be paying any attention to a French cashier in a delicatessen on a side street. And that is when the assassin will strike at LeDuc.'

'Good heavens, Holmes! You have lost none of your skills for want of exercise.'

His eyebrows arched. 'Naturally,' he said. 'I can even tell you the name of the man charged with his murder. He is one Gavrilo Princip.' He produced a photograph of three men in suits sitting on a bench. 'That's Princip on the right.'

Princip looked as if his suit belonged to a man two sizes bigger than him, while his hat seemed too small for his head. His face was chiselled, his moustache thin. He didn't strike fear into my heart and I said so.

'Don't underestimate him. He was trained for the specific purpose of assassination at a revolutionary camp in Serbia. He is in the pay of the Scottish Unionist faction, and his task is to make sure the true king of Scotland never assumes his throne. Our job, Watson, is to ensure he fails.'

We arrived in Sarajevo on the twenty-fourth of June. Its slightly shabby Hapsburg-era buildings gave it the appearance of a run-down Vienna. We found lodgings near the Latin Bridge over the sluggish brown waters of the Milijaka River, close to the delicatessen on the corner of Franz Josef Street where Henri LeDuc was employed. Holmes had assumed the appearance of an unemployed labourer and lounged in an arcade of shops on the other side of the street. I browsed the wares of the delicatessen and managed to eavesdrop on the cashier, who addressed his colleagues in both rapid French and rather more halting Italian. Confirmation came as I perused the unfamiliar cooked meats when I heard one of the servers call a warning to him. 'LeDuc, *prenez garde!*' He stepped neatly aside to avoid a falling package a customer had left precariously on the counter.

Over the next few days, we learned that Henri LeDuc was a creature of habit. He arrived for work promptly at 7.30. At 10.30, he left his position by the counter and crossed the street, where he sheltered in a doorway to smoke two cigarettes. At 1.30, he walked down to the river and sat on a bench to eat an apple and some sort of roast meat patty. He smoked another cigarette on his way back to his post. Three hours later, he took his final cigarette break then at 6, he left Schiller's and walked briskly to a cheap-looking boarding house across the river.

Every evening, he emerged from his lodgings and walked along the river to a large and raucous tavern. Music and laughter spilled on to the quayside and inside was thick with pipe smoke and the smell of fried food. We spotted our quarry at a long table with a dozen other young men drinking beer. LeDuc produced a pack of cards, and half a dozen of the drinkers began to play something that resembled gin rummy. There was nothing remotely regal about LeDuc as he returned later in unsteady fashion to his room. I said as much to Holmes.

'As the proverb has it, Watson, opportunity maketh the man. Once Alexander Stewart and his kinsmen have the grooming of him, King Henry may yet prove a wise and worthy ruler. He has at least learned the ways of the world.'

On the twenty-seventh of June I took up my station on the next bench along from LeDuc's customary picnic spot on Appel Quay. But before he arrived, I noticed another man standing on the quay watching the corner of Franz Josef Street. I was startled by his resemblance to the man in the photograph and I half-rose to my feet before I noticed that beyond him, Holmes himself was on the quayside, hunched over a fishing rod, apparently lost in contemplation of the river. I knew better, however. Nothing would escape his sharp eyes.

Princip, as I believed the man to be, remained in place while LeDuc rounded the corner and settled on his accustomed bench. Unaware of his watchers, he ate quickly and walked back briskly to his post. I saw Holmes toss his fishing rod into the river and replace the cap and muffler he wore with the panama hat which he'd kept rolled up in his pocket.

He straightened up, transformed, and hastened in Princip's wake. I followed more slowly, and saw my friend stroll down the street some way behind the little Serb.

There seemed nothing useful I could do, so I went into Schiller's and joined the queue. I had already discovered their coffee and honey pastries were delicious and I lingered over them as long as I dared. I made sure LeDuc took his afternoon break and then I returned to our lodgings where I wrote a lengthy letter to my wife to pass the time.

It was after midnight when Holmes returned. He smelled of Turkish tobacco and cooking herbs and seemed mightily satisfied. 'Princip may be a trained assassin but he's no detective. He never once looked over his shoulder.'

'Did he follow LeDuc back to his lodgings?'

'He did. And to the tavern. But he made no attempt on LeDuc's life. He is too disciplined to divert from the planned operation. Later, I tracked him to a house on the outskirts of the city where he joined forces with a group of men I take to be his Black Hand associates. I found a vantage point on the balcony of a neighbouring house from where I could see into an upstairs room where they were gathered. On the table their arsenal was laid out – five pistols, three grenades and half a dozen blackjacks.'

'It doesn't seem much weaponry for a revolution,' I said dubiously.

'But enough to generate fear and civil unrest when

the Archduke visits. And to provide perfect cover for the assassination that will earn the cash for more armaments.'

'How will we thwart Princip's plans?'

'I will be at his shoulder from the moment he leaves his lodgings. As soon as he reaches for his pistol, I will strike and prevent him carrying out his task. What he is will then be clear to the police. You, meanwhile, will lead Henri LeDuc to the station, where I will join you. I have cabled Alexander Stewart to await us in Trieste tomorrow to meet his king.'

'But what if LeDuc refuses to accompany me? He may not realise how close he has come to death.'

Holmes gave me a shrewd look. 'Watson, you are a man who inspires trust, not fear.'

I lacked Holmes' certainty, but if all else failed, I would claim to be an emissary from his brother Edouard. I doubted whether news of his death could have reached Henri. He might rage against me afterwards, but the excuse would serve its purpose, I felt moderately confident of carrying out my task successfully.

With our plans in place, I bade Holmes goodnight and took to my bed.

When I woke, Holmes had already departed. I emerged from our lodgings into a very different atmosphere from the previous days. The streets were surprisingly busy for a Sunday morning. In addition to the citizens going about their regular business, the devout in their Sunday best were making their way to and from church and mosque. But everyone's attention was drawn however briefly to the uniformed policemen patrolling the streets between the river and the Town Hall. I felt their eyes slide over me then move on to the next face as I walked along Appel Quay and into Franz Josef Street.

In what had now become habit, I entered Schiller's Delicatessen and joined the queue at the counter. I ordered a coffee and a pastry and retreated to the counter at the rear of the shop to consume them. I had a good view of LeDuc, who was going about his business as usual.

I had barely made inroads into my pastry when a muffled detonation silenced the conversation in the café. There followed loud exclamations in the local tongue and half the patrons rushed into the street. LeDuc paused in his work for a moment, said something to a colleague then returned to totting up bills. A few minutes later, a man dashed back inside and shouted what I presumed to be a report to the room. I stood up and returned to the counter. *'Qu'est que c'est?'* I asked LeDuc.

'Je ne sais pas,' he replied. *'Peut-être une bombe. On a attaque l'Archiduc, on a dit.'*

Whatever had taken place did not seem to have caused undue consternation in Schiller's. Five minutes before LeDuc was due to take his break, I left the delicatessen and crossed the street. Leaning against the wall near LeDuc's favoured doorway, I made a show of cleaning and filling my pipe, all the while scanning the crowds. There was a different air in the street now, a kind of fevered excitement. And the police officers had disappeared, all but a pair who stood on the quay at the end of the street, looking this way and that with an air of confusion.

Still I could not see who I was looking for. Neither Princip nor Holmes was in sight. LeDuc emerged from the delicatessen and made his way to his regular slot, nodding to me as he lit his cigarette.

Of a sudden, I spotted the little Serb assassin turn into Franz Josef Street from the opposite end to the quay. He walked quickly, weaving through the crowded pavement. And at his heels, dressed to blend in with the Sunday passers-by, was Holmes. He appeared to slouch but moved with deceptive speed, keeping only a few feet between himself and Princip.

They were almost level with us when events took an extraordinary turn. A long black Gräf & Stift open sports car, its top folded down, turned into the street. Sitting in the seats behind the driver were a plump man in a grand military uniform topped by a helmet resplendent with plumes of green feathers, and an elegantly dressed woman. The car had no sooner turned into the street than it stopped dead in front of the door of Schiller's. *'Qu'est que c'est? Je pense que c'est l'Archiduc,'* I remarked to LeDuc.

Whatever he replied was lost in the confusion of the moment. As if in slow motion, I saw Princip step forward, reach inside his jacket for a pistol and take aim at the young Frenchman by my side. Before he could pull the trigger, Holmes was upon him. But my friend was thrown off balance by a woman bumping into him from behind. Instead of hurling Princip to the ground, Holmes could only make him stagger. The pistol went off and to my horror I saw a terrible bloom of blood appear on the Archduke's throat.

Princip almost recovered himself and fired wildly in our direction, missing LeDuc for a second time but instead wounding the woman passenger in the abdomen. She fell across the man's legs as their blood mingled in a terrible flow. Holmes fell back, aghast, as Princip put his gun to his own head, but before he could shoot, the bystanders, joined by the two policemen from Appel Quay, fell upon him and disarmed him.

In those few short moments, the history of the world was changed. And all because a driver took a wrong turning.*

---

* Holmes and Watson succeeded in extracting Henri LeDuc from the chaos following the 'assassination' of Archduke Ferdinand, and introduced him to Alexander Stewart in Trieste. Stewart took LeDuc back to Scotland, but the events that followed the death in Sarajevo overtook the Scottish Home Rule Bill and the First World War consigned it to the parliamentary dustbin. History does not record what became of the true king of Scotland, but rumours persist that Henri LeDuc changed his name to Stewart, married a woman from his clan, and fathered several children. If so, the identity of the true monarch of Scotland remains to be revealed.

ANCIENT
AND
MODERN

Alan asked me to marry him right here, on the edge of the cliff. There was a glorious sunset at his back, smudged bars of scarlet and gold and bruised plum, the colours reflected in the ruffled surface of the gunmetal sea. I couldn't see his face because of the radiance behind him and I wondered what he was up to, getting down on one knee on the uneven rock. I thought he'd dropped something. But the next thing I knew was, 'Ellie, will you do me the honour of being my bride?'

I only hesitated because my mouth was too busy grinning. 'You bet,' I yelped. Then I yanked him to his feet and squeezed him so tight his breath exploded in a loud, 'Oof!'

Of course, I never told Colin any of that.

Serendipity. The dictionary defines it as the 'occurrence of events by chance in a happy or beneficial way'. And serendipity was what brought us to this place.

Our summer holiday that year was a cycling tour of the north-west Highlands. We'd driven up from our home in Manchester with the bikes mounted on the back of the car. We left the car in Ullapool and set off. We'd spent weeks planning our routes, poring over maps on the living room table, googling points of interest on the way, deciding on the youth hostels and B&Bs we'd stay in overnight. We'd given the bikes a thorough service and worked out the absolute minimum of packing. We were good at that; it wouldn't be the first time I'd cycled up a hill with a pair of pants pegged across the top of a pannier, drying in the sun.

We were blessed with one of those spells of good weather that makes people agree that if only you could guarantee the sunshine, nobody would ever bother with going abroad. It's a sentiment that resonates even more these days. When I was a kid, Scottish holidays were as memorable for the awfulness of the food as they were for the depressing frequency of the rain. Apart from the glorious fish and chips bought from busy counters in tiny shopfronts filled with the reek of hot fat, mealtimes were an ordeal.

Not these days. That holiday, Alan and I ate like kings. From the pub in the middle of nowhere with dirt-cheap local lobster and chips to the Millionaire Tiffin we picked up from a stall at a village market, we stuffed ourselves with food that brought smiles to our faces. Just as well we were cycling long hours every day or we'd both have come home the size of houses.

That afternoon, we'd fetched up in Lochinver, a village in Sutherland that straggles along the shores of a three-legged inlet of the loch that shares its name. For a small place, it's got a lot of places where you can spend your money. Pubs, restaurants, a bookshop, a pottery, a couple of galleries. And an award-winning pie shop – which as far as we were concerned, meant no contest. I chose pork, chorizo and manchego; Alan went for savoury lamb, on condition we swapped half-way through. We were always good at sharing.

We ate sitting on a bench in the sun, our eyes feasting on a stunning view of twinkling blue water and dramatic rocky shores. Our silence was companionable; although we'd been together for just under five years at that point, we always had plenty to say to each other. We saw a pair of ravens circling and swooping above the rocky point. 'You don't get that in Cheadle,' Alan said.

I laughed. 'You don't get any of this in Cheadle.'

Pies finished, we set off on the last four miles of that day's route. We were booked in for the night at the youth hostel in a tiny hamlet called Achmelvich at the end of a twisting, undulating single-track road. It was hard work in the sunshine, but when we reached our destination, we knew it had been worth every straining turn of the pedals. Achmelvich consisted of a scant handful of croft cottages, the youth hostel and a caravan site. Plus one of the most spectacularly lovely beaches we'd ever seen. We were too early to check in to the hostel, so we locked up our bikes and headed for the sea.

We breasted a low line of dunes then white sand spread before us between the two rocky arms of the bay. The sea glittered in the afternoon light and the soft whisper of waves grew to a gentle shush as we walked down to the water's edge. We walked the length of the bay, rapt. At the far end, a rocky outcrop was hunched above the sand. I could imagine the fun kids would have clambering over it, seeing it as a castle or a pirate ship. But this afternoon, we were the only people around. For the time being, it was our private beach. I couldn't help saying a small prayer of thanks for so special a moment.

At the end of the bay was a gate that led to the caravan site. Alan checked the map and we saw that beyond it lay a headland we could clamber over to look out across the sea towards the Hebrides. There was still plenty of time before we could settle in at the hostel, so we set off across the rocks. 'Lewisian gneiss,' Alan panted, scrambling up an awkward incline. He always knew stuff like that. He was the best man to have on a pub quiz team if you wanted to scoop the rolling jackpot. We had friends who brought him in as a ringer for just those occasions. Mind, as a result there were some pubs in South Manchester we couldn't go back to . . .

There were patches of bog between the rock escarpments and I swear the sheep were laughing at us as we unerringly picked the most awkward route across the rocks, drawn on by the sparkling promise of the sea ahead.

Then we crested a shoulder of the hillside and both stopped in our tracks. Ahead of us, on the edge of the cliff above a steep-banked inlet in the promontory was something so unexpected I wondered if I was hallucinating it. But a quick glance at Alan's face told me he could see it too.

A miniature fortress, geometric concrete shapes

apparently growing out of the rock, topped with what looked like a periscope facing out to sea. There were small square holes in the concrete walls, blank eyes that my imagination filled with gun barrels pointing our way. It was completely incongruous, straight lines against the irregular humps and bumps and treacherous slopes of the rocks.

'What the hell is that?' I said.

'I've no idea.' Alan unfolded the map again. 'There's nothing marked on the map. And I didn't see anything about it when we were checking out our route.'

'Let's take a look.' We descended slowly, fascinated by the sight. I almost missed my footing a couple of times on the way down, so intent was I on our destination. I didn't want to take my eyes off it in case it vanished like Brigadoon.

As we drew closer, it grew less ominous. It was about nine or ten feet tall, and the holes looked as if they'd once held glass bricks. The concrete had been mixed with shells and pebbles from a small shingle beach we could see twenty or so feet below, which added to the camouflage effect of grey concrete in a grey and black and green landscape. From the landward side, there was no obvious entrance, but we could see where a path had been worn round the far corner.

Alan was a couple of steps ahead of me and he called, 'Careful, it's really narrow here, you could easily slip and fall.'

I saw what he meant when I followed him round the corner. The path was barely wide enough to plant my feet side by side. When I looked up, I saw a narrow doorway leading inside the building. Alan had already disappeared inside. The doorway gave on to a narrow passageway that curved round like a snail shell. It was a tight squeeze then suddenly there was a wooden lintel and I was inside a tiny chamber like a monk's cell. 'Wow,' I said, turning around, taking it all in.

Not that there was much to take in. A concrete bed platform with a low lip, just deep enough for a heavy-duty sleeping mat. A fireplace like an oven with pigeonholes alongside it and a ledge, presumably for firewood. Though where you'd find firewood in an area so exposed there were no nearby trees, I had no idea.

'That thing that looks like a periscope? It's the chimney. It's got a right-angle bend at the end to stop the smoke blowing straight back down. That's very clever.' Alan was a builder specialising in sustainable homes; he knew about things like that. 'And that entrance, it's the same thing. Curving round like that means the wind can't blow straight in either.' He nodded, pursing his lips approvingly. 'Very impressive.'

All the same, there was no glass in the windows, no signs of occupation. Nothing except a graffiti tag sprayed across one wall. Not even beer cans and used condoms, which there would have been if this extraordinary structure had been in Cheadle.

'It'd be hard, living here. No running water. Not even a nearby stream. You'd have to carry all your water in with you.'

'Or come in by boat.' I pointed in the direction of the shingle beach. 'You could bring a little boat right up to the shore there. It's not that far.'

Alan laughed. 'Humping water thirty feet up the hillside? Rather you than me. And there's no sanitation.'

'There's the sea.'

'It's not the Med, Ellie. It's the Atlantic. It'd freeze your bits and tits off eleven months of the year.' Then he moved closer and drew me into an embrace. 'Nice and private though,' he muttered between kisses. Then he pulled away and headed back outside. 'Soon be time to get into the hostel,' he said. 'And then we can maybe find out what the hell this is.'

I followed more slowly. I felt a strange attraction to the concrete pillbox on the end of the point. Who had built it? And why? And how come it seemed to be a secret from map-makers and tour guide writers alike?

The hostel was surprisingly quiet, considering the weather. There were three geology students from Edinburgh up to climb Suilven and the three Corbetts of Quinag; a quartet of German bikers; and a pair of sinewy cyclists doing the North Coast 500, a gruelling ride that we'd decided was more pain than pleasure. We'd bought some smoked fish, onions and potatoes in Lochinver earlier and made a basic fish stew, followed by a couple of rhubarb and apple pies from the pie shop.

Later, we sat on a bench outside with a view of the

beach and lured the warden to join us with the half-bottle of Talisker we'd brought with us. He was a big bear of a man in his mid-thirties, shaggy of hair and beard, dressed in a plaid shirt, khaki cargo shorts and a pair of battered work boots. His arms were covered in colourful tattoos in complicated Celtic designs. His name was Martin, and he'd moved up from Tyneside to run the hostel, which seemed to me to be pretty close to the perfect job.

After we got past the preliminaries, I asked the question we really wanted the answer to. 'We walked out to the point this afternoon,' I began. 'What on earth is that concrete pillbox doing out there?'

Martin chuckled. 'So you found the Hermit's Castle?'

'Is that what it's called? What's it for? Who built it?'

'Both good questions. To be honest, the answers are a bit unsatisfactory. But here's how the story goes.' He shuffled around on the bench so he could see us better. 'Back in the early 1950s, a young man arrived here in Achmelvich. An architect from Norwich and, from all accounts, he'd run away from his life because he was having some sort of breakdown.' Clearly, this was not the first time Martin had told his tale. He'd eased into it with all the comfortable familiarity of a favourite armchair.

'He didn't have much to do with the locals. He bought a little open boat down in Lochinver with an outboard motor. And he started buying bags of cement as well as the usual stuff that campers go for – bread, eggs, fish, tea, milk. He had a three-gallon drum of water that he filled up at the fishing pier. And wood. Apparently he bought some fishing boxes from one of the trawlers.'

'Did people not wonder what he was up to?'

Martin shrugged. 'Back then, a lot of the land round here was owned by the kind of absentee landlord who employed people to do all kinds of nonsense. So if they thought about it at all, they just assumed it was another one of the laird's stupid carry-ons. And because he was going in and out by boat, none of the locals really saw anything. You can't see the thing till you're right on top of it. He was camping out there in a tent, out of sight and out of mind.' He chuckled. 'Not just his own mind.'

'I can't believe nobody was curious about what he was up to,' Alan said.

Martin shook his head. 'What you've got to remember, man, is that up here back then, it was like the Middle Ages. It was virtually feudal. The laird was the law and it didn't do to question him. So if a man wasn't causing any bother, best to leave well alone. So your man, he made his frames out of wood from the fish boxes and he cast his concrete and he built his little castle. It took him the best part of six months.' He paused for dramatic effect.

I let him have his moment then said, 'Then what?'

'He slept in it one night, then he went back to Norwich and never came back.'

'I told you,' Alan said. 'No sanitation. The fatal flaw.'

'Or maybe he was cured,' I suggested. 'It was therapy and it worked. He knew he could face the world again.' Then something struck me. 'If he didn't tell people what he was doing, how did they know what he'd done? And that he'd gone home?'

Martin smiled. 'Most people don't ask. I wondered that myself when I first heard the story, but actually the answer's the least interesting part. He sold the boat back to the fisherman he'd bought it from in the first place. He told him what he'd been up to and how he was heading back to Norwich to pick up where he left off.'

'You'd have thought he'd have come back,' Alan said. 'Just to see what had happened to it.'

Martin finished his dram and set the glass down on the bench. 'For all we know, he might have. He might have come back and stayed in this very youth hostel and hiked out to the point to check it out. But if he did, he never let on to anybody round here. Serious walkers and wild campers sometimes use it as a bothy. Who knows? He might have done that for old times' sake.' He stood up and stretched. 'Now I've got my chores to finish before I can call it a day.'

'What time do you lock up?' Alan asked.

'It's supposed to be ten o'clock, but I don't generally bother till getting on for midnight. It stays light so late at this time of year, it seems daft.'

'So if we went out to the point to watch the sunset, we'd still be able to get back in?'

Martin grinned. 'Some nights I don't bother locking up at all. It's not like we're a hotbed of crime out here. Whatever time you come back, it's canny.'

*

So we hiked back out to the point, our path lit by a sunset whose colours ranged dramatically from violet to lemon yellow, shifting with every passing minute, splashing random shades on the rocks and the sea and the etiolated fronds of cloud that drifted lazily across the sky. It was a remarkable show. If we'd filmed it, nobody would have believed it wasn't artificially enhanced.

We sat for a while on the hillside above the Hermit's Castle, then wc walked down. Close up, I could see that there were dozens of little shells incorporated in the concrete. Although it was such an oddity, this geometric outcropping among gneiss that had been shaped and scoured by millennia of weather and wear, the pebbles and shells gave it an unexpected organic connection to the landscape. It was an extraordinary thing to have imagined and then conjured into being, but in a funny kind of way it felt as if it belonged here. Even more oddly, I felt a connection to it too.

So, although I was genuinely gobsmacked when Alan got down on one knee and asked me to marry him, it seemed curiously appropriate. When I pulled him to his feet and hugged him, I'd never been more at home anywhere on earth. We melted into each other's embrace and without discussing it or thinking about it, we slipped inside the Hermit's Castle and fell on each other with an urgency that took no account of hard surfaces or tight corners.

When we surfaced, panting and exhausted, we realised we were losing the light. We hurried back across the treacherously uneven rocks before the dimming of the day made it too perilous to consider. As we walked back up the track to the hostel, we held hands in a tight grip. Something had shifted in our relationship, moving the intensity up a gear. We both knew without the need for words that we'd sealed something out there at the Hermit's Castle. Something that would last a lifetime.

I never told Colin any of that either.

Who knew that a lifetime would be so short?

We never even managed the wedding. Eleven months after the night at the Hermit's Castle, Alan was dead. He was cycling to work, at a site a couple of miles from our home, down the busy A56 near Old Trafford. It's a complicated and confusing series of junctions, and a van driver realised at the last minute he was in the wrong place, so he cut across two lanes of traffic without warning. Brakes screeched, horns blared, but Alan was on the far side of those two lanes, unsighted by a people carrier and he kept going. The van ploughed into him, mangling man and bike, and sliding sideways into a bus shelter.

When the paramedics arrived a startlingly short time later, there was nothing for them to do except pronounce life extinct. For a long time afterwards, I felt my life had gone the same way. Alan was the love of my life. I know it's a cliché but it's also the truth. We shared a sense of humour, an outlook on the world, a common set of values. Our tastes in films and music and books overlapped, but there was enough leeway for each of us to have our own personal preferences that we indulged on our own or with friends. We weren't joined at the hip but there was never a day apart that we wouldn't rather have spent in each other's company.

After he died, bleakness descended on me like a blanket. Not one of those soft snuggly baby blue ones; the rough, prickly grey kind that makes your skin itch. All that kept me going for those first few months was the prospect of the trial. I lived for the day when the man who had destroyed our future would stand in the dock and face the consequences of his recklessness. The police officer I spoke to about making a victim impact statement said that on a charge of causing death by dangerous driving there was a maximum sentence of fourteen years in jail but in this case it would probably be more like eight or nine years. It wasn't a fair exchange for what I'd lost but I decided that I could live with that. So I opted not to make a personal statement because I couldn't face going through everything I'd lost. Not with a stranger.

If I'd known how things would turn out, I'd have poured my heart out on the page and screamed it out in court like a demented fishwife. But I didn't know, and I didn't speak, and maybe things would have been different if I had.

Probably not, though.

*

The first time I saw Colin was in court. I was sitting near the back of the public gallery. Friends had warned me about the way the press would focus in on me and I didn't want to be on show for them. Where I was sitting, it would be an effort for them to turn and stare at me and I thought the judge wouldn't stand for that. So I was sitting anonymously by myself when they led him into the dock.

It was a shock, to see him in the flesh. He didn't look like the photo in the local paper. They'd snatched it on his front step when he opened the door to them and he'd looked unshaven and bleary, like a man struggling to negotiate a major hangover and failing by a mile. Today, though, he was a man scrubbed up for a night out. Clean-shaven; eyes bright and free from dark shadows, unlike mine; dark hair freshly barbered and sleek as a seal's; collar and tie and a suit still pressed from the dry cleaners. He looked more like someone who worked for the legal system than someone who was about to be nailed by it.

Shock enough, you'd think. But there was more to come. And from the least expected direction. The prosecution barrister stood up and told the court that the defendant had agreed to plead guilty to the lesser charge of causing death by careless or inconsiderate driving. In the light of the guilty plea, he went on, he urged the court to sentence him to no more than two years imprisonment.

What had happened to the trial I'd been promised? What had happened to eight or nine years? It made no sense to me. I felt faint and my ears were ringing so loudly I barely heard the judge hand down eighteen months in jail and a two-year driving ban. I felt physically sick and it was all I could do to stand after he'd been led away.

Outside the courtroom, I spotted the policeman I'd spoken to about my victim statement. 'What just happened in there?' I stammered. 'That's not what you told me to expect.'

He had the grace to look ashamed, the colour rising up his neck and into his cheeks. 'I didn't know myself till this morning. His barrister came to the CPS with the offer of a deal. Saves a trial, and that saves money.' His words were bitter and he shook his head, his eyes following the prosecutor as he swept along the hall without a backward glance. 'And that lot can never resist a result they don't have to work for.'

My legs gave way then, and only the strong arms of the policeman saved me from crashing to the marble floor. He steered me to a bench and sat with me while I tried to make sense of what had happened. The life of the man I loved had been bartered away for next to nothing, for the convenience of the court. Nobody gave a damn about Alan. What was the death of one good man weighed against saving the system a few quid?

The next time I saw Colin was almost a year later, spotting for a gym bunny doing bench presses. Ten months in a low-security jail didn't seem to have caused him much grief. He'd bulked out through the shoulders and the legs from working out in the prison gym and, I guessed, in his cell. According to my friendly police liaison officer, Colin had walked straight into his job at the gym when he walked out of jail because his uncle was the franchise owner.

I signed up for a year's membership. I was willing to play the long game. I didn't think there was any chance of Colin recognising me. Since the trial and the handful of blurred photos in the press, I'd had my hair cut; I'd had laser surgery so I didn't need glasses any more; and I'd lost so much weight I'd had to buy a whole new wardrobe. Grief seems to take you one of two ways. Alan's sister went in for comfort eating and ballooned three stone. I lost all interest in food and only ate because the alternative was falling over.

I chose Colin to perform my gym induction and set my exercise regime. I didn't flirt. I forced myself to talk to him in a relaxed and friendly way. Deferred to his knowledge and admired his skills. Over the next three months, I found excuses to talk to him about my programme, my goals and my achievements. Gradually, we became more friendly, both of us telling only part of the truth about ourselves. Both lying, though for very different reasons.

In the fourth month, having established his taste for The 1975, I turned up at the gym with a pair of tickets for a gig in Leeds later that week. 'I was going with my pal Denise, but her mum's gone into hospital and she's had to go back to Stoke to take care of her dad,' I said.

'Then I remembered you saying you like them, and I wondered if you wanted the spare ticket?'

Of course he did. He even offered to drive us over the Pennines for our night out.

I won't pretend it was easy to go through with it. There wasn't a moment when I let go the knowledge that I was with the man who had taken Alan from me. At one point I had to go to the loo and throw up, I was so disgusted with myself for being there with him. But I had a plan. The long game. Whatever it took.

And six months later, there I was in the north-west Highlands again. Not a cycling holiday this time. No, we were driving round, Colin and me. Taking our time, staying in B&Bs, going for walks. My flesh still crept when he touched me but I was used to it by then and I could fake it better than any BAFTA-toting actress.

One night we stayed in Ullapool. Fish and chips and a walk along the harbour. Whisky nightcaps in a busy bar. Then up the next morning and a walk up towards the Falls of Kirkcaig. We didn't go all the way; Colin was plagued by the midges and anyway, in spite of the muscles and the gym, he's not really that fit when it comes to beasting up hills.

We'd booked in at the Culag Hotel in Lochinver, but I suggested a drive up to Achmelvich. 'There's an amazing building right out on the point. It's only a short walk out of the village but you'd never know it's there.' And I told him the story. 'I went there

141

once with a friend of mine, years ago. I'd love to show it to you.'

Colin grumbled a bit, and my heart was in my mouth in case he refused. But he gave in. Appropriately, it was another spectacular sky that greeted us when we got out of the car, but this time it wasn't glorious colours but dramatic storm clouds rolling in. 'Are you sure about this?' he said. 'It looks like it's going to chuck it down.'

'That's miles away out at sea,' I reassured him. 'We'll be there and back before the first spit of rain.'

We scrambled over the rocks. I led the way; I remembered it so well from before. Colin trailed behind, occasionally muttering when he planted his foot in a suck of bog, or slipped on a treacherous piece of rock. And then we crested the final hillock and there it was. The Hermit's Castle.

'Wow,' he said.

Thank goodness, I thought.

We scrambled down and I pointed out the shells and pebbles embedded in the concrete.

'Amazing,' he said.

We rounded the corner of the building, heading for the doorway. I let Colin go ahead of me and just at the narrowest part of the path, I called his name. He half-turned, awkward in the narrow space. I swung my arm back and smashed him in the side of the head with the sharp-edged chunk of stone I'd picked up on the beach at Ullapool.

I saw the blood on his temple and the shock in his

eyes as he staggered, his arms windmilling helplessly. A small push in the chest was all it took to finish the job. He tumbled backwards down the cliff, head first, bouncing off the unforgiving ancient Lewisian gneiss. He didn't even cry out.

I peered over the edge. He was sprawled at the water's edge, his head half-submerged. I'd checked the tide tables and I knew the high tide would cover him within the hour. I settled down to wait, my back against the unyielding concrete of the Hermit's Castle, watching the storm rolling ever closer.

In spite of its modernity, it inhabits a primitive place, a place of rock and water. Modern justice failed me, so I reverted to the primitive kind. 'Thou shalt give life for life, eye for eye, tooth for tooth, hand for hand, foot for foot, burning for burning, wound for wound, stripe for stripe.' Amen to that, Colin.

THE
DEVIL'S
SHARE

The rocks were slippery with spray from the high waterfall. The brown water, broken white by the height of the cascade, gleamed and glistened and glittered, the same colour as the whisky that emerges from the other end of the distilling process. The three youngsters clambered hesitantly up the steep hillside, stopping frequently to catch their breath. They were accustomed to being out of the city, to running wild through the landscape. But their usual landscape was tamer than the wildness of Jura. They'd learned their freedom on sand dunes and waymarked woodland paths, not this raw world of rock and heather, bracken and pines, sudden flows and pools of water. Here, it was easy to lose any sense of direction. To a stranger, one stalking moor looks much like another. To a newcomer, all of the three breast-shaped Paps look the same. A recipe for disorientation.

Nervous of this, Jack kept checking over his shoulder to make sure of his bearings. He understood that being eldest meant he'd carry the blame if anything went sour. But so far, everything was sweet. He could see the slate roof of the four-square Georgian lodge next to the distillery and beyond that, the Bay of Small Isles, a couple of small yachts bobbing at anchor. At dinner the night before, they'd watched the boats sail in to the sheltered anchorage. He'd been glad they were staying in the lodge and not confined on a boat at the mercy of unpredictable weather and queasiness. Much better to be able to walk out the front door and feel solid ground under your feet.

And then the ground shifted beneath him. A yell, almost a scream, rose above the roar of the water. Jack whirled round, just in time to catch the final moment of Cameron's tumble from the rocks into the cascade. Jack's imagination leapt ahead and for a moment he couldn't work out why his cousin's body wasn't being tossed down the waterfall, at the mercy of the joint forces of water and gravity. But Cameron had apparently disappeared. The screaming Jack could hear now came from his sister Roisin, still clinging to the rocks but reacting as if she was the one in trouble.

Jack carefully picked his way back down to his sister's side and shouted, 'Where's Cameron?'

She stopped screaming long enough to give him a look of contemptuous dismissal. 'He's in the waterfall.'

'How can he be *in* the waterfall?'

She shrugged. 'I don't know. But he fell in and he didn't come out so he must still be in there, right? I mean, it's not like it's a portal to another dimension, is it?'

Jack looked at the tumbling water. For all he could see of his cousin, Roisin's sarcasm could have hit the mark. He stared intently into the water, willing Cameron to appear. When he saw a flicker of red, he wondered momentarily whether he'd wished it into being. Then he saw it again, and this time he was sure it was Cameron's T-shirt. 'Look, there he is,' he cried. 'There must be a ledge or a cave or something. Roisin, go back down for help.'

For once, she didn't need telling twice. Jack watched her scrambling descent, willing her not to fall and double his problems. Once she disappeared, cut off from him by the distillery buildings and the lodge below, he turned back to the waterfall. Yes, he could definitely catch glimpses of the shirt. And it looked like Cameron was moving around, so he absolutely wasn't dead or seriously injured. Jack settled on a rock to wait, arms curled round his bent legs, his body folded tight against itself, holding in the fear.

The rescue seemed to take no time at all. Within minutes of Roisin disappearing, bodies had emerged on the hillside, swarming up the rocks, sure-footed and serious, bred-in-the-bone Diurachs and incomers both. Nicol the boatman reassured Jack with a friendly arm round his shoulders while others roped themselves into a human chain and moved into the turbulent water. Their approach was cautious without being tentative and sooner than seemed possible, they were backing out of the broken wall of water with Cameron's skinny body clamped round the leader like a baby spider monkey.

With perfect timing, the mothers arrived. The burly man who had led the rescue peeled Cameron off and passed him to his mother. She hugged him close, both shivering with shock and relief. Past fear now, he loosened his grip and half-turned towards the waterfall. 'There's a barrel of whisky in there,' he said.

The Diurachs exchanged doubtful looks then turned their faces towards Willie Cochrane, the Glaswegian distillery manager. He shook his head. 'That cannae be right. We can account for every cask. Customs and Excise make sure of that.'

Cameron's smile was conciliatory. 'No, really. Honestly. There's a barrel just like the ones you showed us in the warehouse.'

'There's only one way to find out,' Nicol said, looking expectantly at the rescuers.

The leader shrugged. 'Why not? We're already wet. Anybody got a light?'

One lad had a rubber-encased torch clipped to his belt. He handed it over without a word and the men stepped back under the battering shower of the waterfall.

While the mothers fussed over Cameron, everyone else milled around making a meal of doing nothing useful. They didn't have long to wait. The men emerged, backing out of the water and shaking themselves like dogs. 'The boy's right,' the leader said. 'I've no bloody idea how they got it up there, but there's a wee cave in the rocks, hardly room to stand up in. And right at the back, there's a whisky barrel.'

'That cannae be,' Willie repeated, shaking his head vigorously. 'No way.'

'It's no' your problem, Willie,' the man said. 'It's a 1901 cask.'

Incredulity widened Willie's eyes. A broad grin spread across his small features. 'You're kidding me.'

'I'm telling you. It must have been one of the last casks out of the old distillery before they closed it down.'

Willie rubbed his hands. A 111-year-old whisky; he could see the pound signs already. 'So, how do we get it out of there?' he said.

Archie Maclean liked to sit by the window. His cottage was tucked away at the end of a track, the best thing about it the view of the raised beach above Loch Tarbert. Mostly the only sounds were the sea and the birds, except when the choppers came clattering in with VIP guests ferried up for a bit of stalking and shooting on Lord Astor's estate. That was one of the few things that had changed in this corner of the island since he was a boy. Ninety-two now, with plenty of aches and pains to prove it. But he didn't feel close to death.

Jura had a tradition of longevity. Some scientist had told them it was something to do with high levels of selenium in the water. Archie thought it was most likely because of clean air, hard but simple living and decent whisky. For years, they'd had to rely on friends and family across the narrow strait on Islay for a reliable supply of a good dram, but since the distillery had started up again forty years before, there had been no shortage among the locals.

He checked his watch. In ten minutes, he'd turn the radio on to catch the national news. Getting old didn't mean you had to give up on understanding the world. Once a week, his great-grandson Callum took him down to the Service Point at Craighouse where he could use the internet to email his son in New Zealand and his daughter in Spain. Archie liked to browse the web too, following links into strange nooks and crannies of cyberspace.

A couple of guillemots caught his eye and he followed their flight across the loch and out of sight. An unexpected sound made him cock his head to one side, straining to make it out. Then he relaxed. Callum's Land Rover, its clapped-out diesel engine coughing up the track. Archie smiled and pushed up on the arms of his chair, creaking to his feet and heading for the kitchen. He liked that Callum stopped in for these unscheduled visits. Archie didn't want his family to come by out of obligation. He'd rather be on his own than feel like a charitable deed. But he'd always had a special bond with Callum, the eldest of his generation.

The engine cleared its throat and died away. Archie felt the cool air of the afternoon as the door opened and Callum strode in. He gave Archie's thin shoulders a squeeze on his way to one of the kitchen chairs.

'Your hair's wet,' Archie said.

'Nothing gets past you, Daddo. You'll never believe what we've been up to.' Callum shook his big head, the shaggy reddish hair falling in damp locks to his shoulders.

'Try me.' Archie put teabags in mugs and poured boiling water on them.

'You know the river that comes down from the Market Loch?'

'The whisky river?' Archie stirred the brew and carefully lifted the bags out, laying them on a saucer he left by the kettle for that purpose.

'Aye. Well, one of the bairns on holiday at the lodge fell into the waterfall this morning, so we had to go in after him. Because he'd disappeared. Like magic.'

Startled, Archie slopped tea on the table. Callum jumped up and fetched a cloth, cleaning the spillage while the older man groped for a chair and sat heavily. 'A cave?' His voice was weak and querulous.

'Aye, a cave. Good guess, Daddo.'

'Ach, that hillside's got a fair few caves dotted about. It's no' rocket science.'

'So, it's a cave. We get the bairn out, no bother. But he starts going on about a cask of whisky in the cave. Willie was there, and he was adamant it couldnae be one of his. But the bairn was just as adamant about what he'd seen. So, more to humour him than anything else, we went back in. And right enough, there was a barrel.'

Archie sipped his tea hoping it would ease the nausea churning his stomach. 'That's amazing,' he said, sounding anything but amazed.

'But Willie was right, it wasnae one of his barrels. Guess what it was?'

'I don't know.' Archie stared into his tea. 'From Islay?' It was a reasonable guess – at any given time over the past century there had been at least half a dozen distilleries on the island across the narrow strait from Jura.

153

'Better than that. It's a 1901 barrel from the old Jura distillery itself. Willie was about passing out with the excitement.'

'Aye? I bet he was.'

Callum took a healthy swig of tea. 'Christ knows how they got it up there in the first place.'

'They'll never get it down again, surely?' Archie sounded nonchalant, but his lumpy arthritic fingers clutched his mug close to his chest.

Callum tapped the side of his nose. 'Know-how, that's what it takes. Norman Shaw had the very thing on the boat. A big tripod for a block and tackle. The lads lashed the barrel with ropes and guided it out through the rocks, then Norman let it down the slope bit by bit. We had one or two hairy moments, but nobody got hurt and neither did the barrel. Amazing sight, Daddo. You could still make out the writing on the barrel end – "Jura 1901".'

'So where's the barrel now?'

'Willie and his crew huckled it away into the bond. I mean, technically it doesn't belong to the distillery, but nobody wants to get into a *Whisky Galore* scenario with the exciseman. The bond seemed like the best solution. Willie's going to broach the cask tomorrow and see what the whisky is like. If it's any good at all, he'll get the master blender over from the mainland. See, if it's special, Willie says it'll be sold for a lot of money and we'll all get a cut. Once Robert Paterson's given it the stamp of approval, the sky's the limit.'

Archie stared over Callum's shoulder at the corner

of Loch Tarbert visible through the kitchen window. 'I've got a feeling it'll be special, all right.'

Callum finished his tea and stood up. 'I hope so. I could do with a few bob. Get some work done on the Land Rover. And maybe a new outboard for the dinghy.' He patted Archie on the shoulder. 'I'll see you on Thursday, Daddo. Usual time, eh?' Lost in his dreams of engines, he didn't notice Archie's failure to say farewell.

What would a body look like after sixty-four years steeped in whisky in an oak cask? Archie had once found a forensic anthropology forum where some American professor answered people's questions. Some of the things they wanted to know were worryingly bizarre. 'What would a pubic scalp in a jar of formalin look like?' one had wanted to know. 'Tinned tuna, with hair,' had been the laconic response.

He'd come back a couple of weeks later and asked, 'What would a body look like if it had been in a barrel of whisky for fifty years?'

The answer had appeared almost immediately.

'Your body would be perfectly preserved, provided he was completely covered by the alcohol,' the professor had written. 'Everything would be as is, inside and outside the body. You'd even have the stomach contents perfectly preserved so you could tell what he ate for his last meal fifty years before. There would only be one major change. Just as whiskey gets its colour from the wood it's matured in, so your guy would have taken on the same colouration. If he started out a white man, he's going to be pretty damn dark after fifty years. Even the whites of his eyes will have changed colour – he's going to look jaundiced at the very least.'

It wasn't the answer he'd expected. He'd thought the whisky would be more like acid, slowly eating the body away. He'd been convinced that after all this time, there would be nothing left of Jock Lindsay except some sediment at the bottom of the barrel. The notion that he was hanging there, suspended like a museum specimen, was unsettling. Still, Archie had told himself, the cave and its secret had been undisturbed for more than half a century. The chances were it would stay that way until he was long gone. These days, he doubted there was anyone else left who could put a name to the dead man.

Archie washed the mugs and set them on the drainer. There was another helping of his granddaughter's venison casserole in the fridge. He'd been planning on having it with a few potatoes and carrots for his tea. But he wasn't in the mood. Instead, he filled his battered hip flask with sixteen-year-old Jura, put on his old tweed stalking jacket and headed out the door, leaning heavily on his walking stick.

He took his time walking down to the raised beach, where he settled on his usual flat-topped boulder. These days, there was no padding on his bony backside and he knew he wouldn't be able to sit for long. At least the midges had given up on him. Nothing left to suck out of him, he often thought. Archie unscrewed his flask and sipped at the warm peaty drink. He could feel the heat all the way down to his stomach. 'Make the most of it,' he said out loud.

A faint breeze ruffled the inlet of the loch that lapped down below. From here, he could see a couple of the trig points that formed the ingenious navigation system set up in the 1960s to ease the treacherous passage up the snaking waterway that led from the sea to the Loch Tarbert anchorage. Before that, the rocky shallows had ripped the bottom out of plenty of strangers' boats. And a few locals who'd grown too cocksure as well.

Back in 1948 there had been no trig points. Just a couple of painted rocks to show the way. It had been a simple job to cover the painted rocks with sacks and paint a couple of decoys. Archie had known that would be enough to confound Jock Lindsay. Although Jock had grown up on Jura he'd cleaved to the land, not the sea. He might have managed to steer his boat up the loch if everything had been where it was supposed to be, but Archie had put paid to that. The motorbike Jock had been carrying on board had made certain his boat would sink as soon as it was holed. Struggling to shore in the dark, weighed down by heavy boots and clothes, Jock had been no match for Archie. Archie had known he'd need every ounce of that advantage; Jock was bigger and tougher and more ruthless than he'd ever been. But he'd been determined to stop Jock. And if that meant stooping to dirty tricks, so be it.

It had ended in murder but it had begun in the schoolroom. Archie and Jock had attended the village school together and when war had broken out, they'd enlisted together, both joining the Parachute Regiment. They'd both had the kind of war that makes a man glad to be alive and whole. Archie knew Jock had seen and done worse than he'd had to deal with. That meant it had been very bad indeed.

After the war, Jock had stayed on in the Army, but Archie had been desperately grateful to return to Jura. He'd found work on the Ardlussa estate in the north of the island, turning his hand to whatever was needed. When the Fletchers had let Barnhill to Eric Blair, the writer the world knew as George Orwell, he'd been told to do what he could to help out but to make it as discreet as possible. He'd done his best, and although Mr Blair's sister had a tongue on her that would strip paint if she was crossed, Archie kept his head down and tried to stay invisible when Mr Blair was up and about.

But mostly, the writer did what writers do. He stayed in his room and hammered away on a typewriter. Sometimes when Archie was crossing the garden, he could hear the clatter of the keys punctuated by the wee tinkle of the carriage return bell, then a salvo of coughing would interrupt the process.

Archie had never been much of a reader but he knew that Mr Blair's books were supposed to be important. He was all for the working man, apparently, though Archie never managed to have any kind of conversation with him. He'd written some book where the animals took over, but it wasn't really about the animals, it was about Communism. It had sold a lot of copies, according to Mrs Fletcher down at the big house.

Miss Blair said the book her brother was writing now would be even more remarkable. She was a wee bit vague on the details, but she did say it would be very political and it would make a lot of people very angry. 'Especially the silly beggars who think that just because the Russians were on our side during the war that they're the sort of people we want to have as allies now it's all over,' she'd said primly one afternoon when they'd been earthing up the potatoes.

Everything had been going fine for Archie. The work at Ardlussa and Barnhill was hard, but he'd got the tenancy of a decent cottage, he'd married Morna Stewart and their first child was on the way. And then he'd had a postcard from Jock Lindsay.

'I'm coming home on leave. See if you can get to Craighouse on Saturday, we'll have a drink.'

Archie wasn't bothered about going drinking with Jock Lindsay. He could think of better ways to spend his money. But Morna picked up the card and nudged him. 'Go on, Archie. You work hard, you deserve a wee bit of fun.'

'I get plenty of fun with you.'

She giggled. 'There's more to life than an Inverlussa ceilidh. Speak to Mrs Fletcher. I'm sure there'll be something needing taking down on the lorry to Craighouse. Or fetching back.'

And so he'd gone.

They'd had a couple of pints in the bar, then Jock had led Archie out on to the pier, producing a flat half-bottle from inside his battledress. He pulled out the cork and passed the bottle to Archie. 'Help yourself,' he urged. 'It's the good stuff from Islay.'

Archie took a tentative sip. The phenolic taint of heavily peated, oily spirit filled his mouth, clearing out his sinuses and making his head swim. 'Christ, Jock, that's some dram,' he said.

'Contacts, Archie. Contacts.'

They walked in silence to the end of the pier, passing the bottle back and forth between them. Finally, Jock turned to face Archie and said, 'So you're working for George Orwell.'

'We call him by his real name. Eric Blair. But aye, that's the way of it.'

'The people I work for, they don't think much of your Mr Blair.'

'Is that right? And who do you work for, Jock? I thought you were a soldier?'

'I am, Archie. But things are not as simple as they were when you wore the uniform. Back then, the enemy was obvious. Now, sometimes the enemy's well hidden.'

'How is Mr Blair anybody's enemy? He just writes books.'

Jock chuckled, a low menacing sound. 'Books that change people's minds, Archie. Books that twist the truth and tell lies. Your Mr Blair, he talks about being for the working man. He claims he's a socialist. But his last book made a mockery of socialism. It made the working man look like a fool. And the word is that he's writing a book now that will turn people away from the left. And where does that leave us? It leaves us puppets of America, that's what. The only thing that will keep us safe is the balance of power, and if we turn our face away from Russia, then we've thrown in the towel. We've traded our sovereignty for Uncle Sam's bribery.'

Archie shook his head, bewildered. He'd never heard Jock talk like this. Nobody from here talked like this. 'Balance of power.' 'Sovereignty.' 'Uncle Sam's bribery.' That was the kind of thing politicians talked about on the radio, not what your pals talked about on a Saturday night out.

'You've grown awfu' political,' he said.

'The people I work for, they've shown me how the world works, Archie.'

Archie scratched his chin. 'Is that right?'

'Archie, you know me. We've been in tight corners together. You know you can trust me.' Jock sounded confident, nudging Archie's arm as he passed the bottle.

'Trust you how?'

'I've got a mission,' Jock said. 'Orders from on high. They don't want your Mr Blair's new book to see the light of day. I hear he's very ill?'

Reluctantly, Archie nodded. 'Aye. There's nothing of him. I sometimes think another winter will see him off. But he's a tough old bird. You never know with his kind.'

Jock took out a pack of cigarettes and offered one to Archie, who shook his head. He'd never taken to tobacco, something he was glad of when he heard Mr Blair's racking cough echo across the garden. A real smoker's cough, that was. Jock lit his own fag then said, 'I've been ordered to destroy the manuscript of this new book. Whatever it takes.'

The words lay between them like a stone. Archie didn't know anything about books but he knew plenty about hard work. And he understood the physical cost to Mr Blair of writing the book that, according to his sister, was close to being finished. 'Is that why you're here?'

Jock laughed. 'No. I'm here because I need help from an old comrade in arms. When I come back, I'll need someone who knows the lie of the land to get me into Barnhill without raising the alarm. In and out, nobody any the wiser. And a good job done without any bother. That's where you come in, Archie.'

Archie shook his head. 'I can't do that. They've been very decent to me.'

Jock suddenly gripped his arm. 'This isn't about you, Archie. This is for your country. Your patriotic duty. See this uniform? It's the same one we both wore to fight the Nazis. These battles now, they're just as important. If you don't help me, it's a kind of treason, Archie.'

Put like that, it was hard to argue against. Jock had always had a forceful personality. By the end of the half-bottle, they'd agreed on the date. Jock, ever confident, said he'd bring a boat up Loch Tarbert. After all, it was the only anchorage on the island that was sheltered from passing boats or road vehicles. Jock would have a motorbike on board. He'd pick up Archie, who would ride pillion. They'd drive as near as they dared to Barnhill, then Archie would lead Jock to the farmhouse. 'I'll take you to the foot of the stairs and no further,' Archie had said. It was the one point on which he wouldn't give way.

But Jock had been relaxed about it. Now he saw the way clear to his objective, he was restored to his usual expansive self. Archie hid his unease but it was still there, burning and grumbling in his stomach like a bad pint.

In the morning, driving back to Ardlussa, squinting against the dull headache the drink had left in its wake, Archie pondered what Jock had told him. The more he thought about it, the more naïve he felt. Jock had sold him a tale about destroying a manuscript. But that was pointless while the author of that manuscript still lived. And he knew Jock well enough to believe he'd never leave a job half-done. That 'whatever it takes' of Jock's had been sufficiently explicit to men who'd been through what they'd seen and done in the war.

It wouldn't be hard to kill Eric Blair, a man weakened and diminished by his illness. A pillow over his face, his body pinned by Jock's superior weight, and it would all be over in minutes. No struggle to wake the house. Nobody would think twice about it, given how ill Mr Blair had been. And the manuscript burned in the fireplace – the act of a man who knew himself to be at death's door, a man dissatisfied with the quality of his work. That was a scenario that made a lot more sense than Jock's nonchalant destruction of a manuscript.

Archie knew he couldn't live with such an outcome. Jock might claim his bosses were patriots, but this wasn't a patriotism Archie recognised. It wasn't what he'd fought for.

And so he made his choice.

What to do with Jock's body was the only thing that made him fret. He didn't want to leave it to the sea loch because it would eventually turn up somewhere. No, let Jock's paymasters wonder what had gone wrong. If they couldn't figure that out, it might keep them from trying again.

It was a problem that nagged him for days. He knew from his wartime experiences that bodies had a way of reappearing. He didn't want that to happen with Jock. He didn't want that hanging over his daily life. He wanted Jock out of sight and out of mind permanently. Archie dug potatoes and staked beans, gralloched deer and rowed out in the insect-thick dusk to fish, but always, he was worrying away at the problem. Soon he would run out of time.

Ironically, it was Mr Blair himself who gave him the

key. Archie had been shifting boulders all day, trying to reshape a field so it would be easier to plough. Blair had walked down from the house towards the end of the afternoon. 'If you'd like a brandy when you're finished, come up to the house. It's all we've got, I'm afraid. If we still had a distillery on the island, I'd be able to offer you a whisky,' he'd said.

And then Archie knew what to do with Jock Lindsay's body.

His father had been working at the old distillery when it had closed down in 1901. Angry locals had removed half a dozen casks from the bonded store and hauled them up into the caves on the hill above the distillery. Over time, the contents had been shared out among the workers. But somebody talked when they shouldn't have and Craighouse had a surprise visit from the exciseman. Archie's father and his pals had shifted the last remaining cask into a cave beside the waterfall. And then one of the idiots had tried to camouflage it further by shifting some of the rocks.

The resulting rock fall left the barrel more or less inaccessible. Over time, people forgot about it. There was enough contraband whisky making its way over from Islay for there to be no burning need for a cask of not very good Jura whisky, even if it was free.

So Archie borrowed one of the horses from Ardlussa and headed down to Craighouse with a sack of potatoes to sell. Late that evening, he found a way through the water to the cave. The cask was still there, damp but unbroached. He'd brought hammer and chisel so he could remove the barrel end. By the light of a torch held in his teeth, he prised open the oak cask, almost knocked back on his heels by the pungent wave of peaty spirit when the wooden disc came free. The cask was still almost full, having lost only a small percentage of its contents to natural evaporation. The angels' share, the distillers called it. Jock would displace a serious amount of whisky, but there would be enough left to submerge him once Archie had rammed him inside.

Four days later, Archie proved his hypothesis. Carrying Jock up the steep hillside had nearly killed him, but fear of the hangman's rope had spurred him on. It was, after all, no different from carrying wounded comrades back to the medics. Easier, in fact, because there was no fear of enemy snipers or mines underfoot.

The struggle to get them both into the cave was risky and terrifying, but Archie was determined. He slid the body into the cask and pushed down, soaking himself in the pungent malt whisky up to the armpits. The whisky sloshed around his feet, disappearing quickly into the earthen floor of the cave. Jock seemed to fold like a concertina into the cask, his back and knees wedging him tight into the staves. And yes, there was plenty of whisky to cover him. The cask was full to the brim again.

Archie dropped the lid back in place. He'd helped himself to a tube of RTV sealant from the boathouse at Ardlussa and he carefully squeezed the compound into the gaps he'd chiselled out of the lid to free it from the staves. When he'd done, he ran his thumb over the joints, making sure they were properly sealed. Then he moved to the very edge of the cave and let the water thunder down over him. It was like being struck by a hundred hands, but he knew it would cleanse him of the whisky. And of any blood that had leaked from Jock's head wound.

Afterwards, that he seemed to be able to put the whole business out of his mind shocked Archie. But it was true. When he remembered that night, it always came as a surprise. Almost as if it had happened to someone else. He didn't live in constant fear of the cask being discovered. He didn't shy away from speculation about what Jock Lindsay might be up to these days. He didn't wake in the night hearing the iron bar smash Jock's skull with a sound like a melon hitting a stone floor.

He didn't even take particular pride in the success of *Nineteen Eighty-Four*, Mr Blair's acclaimed novel. Never even read it. Archie just got on with his life, a well-respected member of the community. A decent husband, father, grandfather and great-grandfather. If anyone had thought to ask, his family would have said he'd had a pretty uneventful life.

And now all that was about to end. Somewhere down the line, some smart forensic scientist would identify Jock Lindsay. Military records would tie him to Archie and there would be a knock at the door. Archie didn't have it in him to lie, not confronted with a direct question. At least Morna was long away to a place where his past couldn't hurt her.

On Thursday, when Callum's Land Rover drew up at the cottage, Archie was already at the door, breathing in the familiar air. But Callum was too full of his own news to register surprise. As soon as he was within hailing distance, he said, 'You'll never guess what's happened! Willie Cochrane hammered a spigot into the whisky cask they found in the waterfall. But there was more than whisky in the barrel – there was a body. A man with his head smashed in. Can you believe it?' He spread his arms in an expansive gesture of amazement.

'I know,' Archie said.

'Did somebody phone you and tell you?' Callum looked disappointed. Then he brightened up. 'Willie said, "at least they didn't spoil a cask of the good stuff". Because apparently, the old distillery malt wasnae up to much.'

Archie nodded. 'So I've heard. I wonder, Callum, could we go some place different today?'

Callum frowned. 'Not the Service Point? How not? Where do you want to go?'

'We'll need to go across to Islay. To the police station. There's something I need to tell them.'

GHOST
WRITER

Gavin Blake had always wanted to be a writer. He couldn't remember a time when that hadn't been his goal. As he'd grown older, he had refined the ambition slightly. What he actually wanted was to make a living from the writing of fiction. He'd watched too many documentaries and attended too many literary events to crave the public life of a writer. He had no desire for the festival performances and signing queues, the Twittersphere or the Radio 4 commentariat. Gavin dreamed instead of days spent in front of a computer screen, fingers flying over the keys, mind blank of anything other than the breathless sequence of words. He visualised his name on book jackets, review pages and bestseller lists, not in the *Guardian*'s 'Comment is free' columns or the *Radio Times* listings.

He prepared himself for his future career by consuming as much fiction as he could cram inside his head. Until his mid-teens, he read indiscriminately. He borrowed from libraries, he spent his pocket money at the second-hand bookstall on the market, he shoplifted new hardbacks from Waterstones. Gradually, with some help from his English teacher, he began to refine his palate, learning to read critically and to identify good prose from dross.

Thanks to hard practice and concentration, by the time Gavin hit his mid-twenties, he could turn a decent sentence. His style flowed smoothly, his language was lucid and often startlingly apt. His dialogue was an authentic replica of the real thing. His characters assumed a life that lingered in the mind like the smile on the Cheshire Cat.

There was only one problem. Gavin had no narrative gift. Story eluded him. Sometimes he sensed it almost within his grasp but whenever he tried to corner it, it slipped away, slithering under his outstretched arms or between his legs like a nutmegging football. Herding cats or wrestling water would have been a simpler alternative for Gavin. Friends suggested remedies. One offered up poetry. Gavin was convinced his imagination was too prosaic. Another suggested literary fiction, given how little it demanded by way of narrative. But Gavin obstinately stuck to his guns. He'd grown to love stories and that was what he wanted to write. He'd just have to try harder, that was all. Read more, learn more, practise more.

It wasn't only his spare time that was devoted to the dark art of narrative. Gavin had learned Mandarin at school and continued his study of Chinese language at university. Now he eked out a living translating Chinese fiction into English, revelling in that literature of vagabonds and thieves, outsiders and dark side entrepreneurs that had found an audience among younger English-speaking readers. He envied the rich drama they brought into his life and coveted the apparent ease and brio of the storytelling. He hoped it would rub off on him. But nothing changed. Still the stories refused to take shape under his hand.

One afternoon, he was ordering up a new Chinese novel at the counter of the university library when a stack of pamphlets caught his eye. 'Creative Writing: Extramural Courses' was superimposed over a romantic sepia photograph of a hand holding a quill pen, apparently composing a Shakespearian sonnet on vellum. Gavin's first reaction was scorn. Who were they trying to kid? A squalid bedsit where an unshaven wretch hunched over a laptop would have been a more accurate representation of the wannabe writer. That or a woman of a certain age with an uncertain smile and a woolly hat. But still, he picked it up and tucked it inside the cover of the book as he carried it back to his seat, not wanting anyone to witness his moment of weakness.

Under cover of his book, he checked out the list of courses on offer. There was nothing humble about the titles: *Mastering the Art of Memoir, Mastering the Art of Lyric Poetry, Mastering the Art of the New Gothic.* And finally, tucked away at the end like the mad aunt on the Christmas card list, *Mastering the Art of Storytelling.* Gavin bit his lip. It held out a promise that was hard to resist. 'A twelve-week evening class anatomising story structure and revealing the tricks of the narrative trade. For the beginning writer struggling with plot, story and theme. Led by distinguished thriller writer Charles Arthur.' Gavin wasn't entirely sure you could be distinguished *and* a thriller writer, but he was willing to suspend his cynicism. He'd read a Charles Arthur novel once. It had been one of half a dozen books abandoned in a holiday cottage. The prose hadn't been up to much, but Gavin remembered the story had hurtled from twist to twist, unlikely events stitched together with a skill that produced the appearance of sense. Perhaps Charles Arthur was exactly what he needed.

There were sixteen of them. Usually when confronted by strangers, Gavin's primary directive was to add to his mental database of characters by cataloguing appearance, accent, verbal idiosyncrasies and physical habits. But that Tuesday evening, he deliberately put that on hold so he could cling fast to Charles Arthur's every word. It didn't take Gavin long to realise that 'call me Charlie' employed a teaching technique often assumed by those who don't actually have that much to say. Charlie made the most of his insights by repeating everything at least four times. First he delivered the straightforward statement. Then he elaborated on it in slightly different terms. Next came a second variation. Then finally, he'd return to the first bald statement. Once the methodology became clear to Gavin and he understood he only had to listen to a quarter of Charlie's words of wisdom, he relaxed and allowed himself to check out his fellow students.

He didn't get far. He nailed the salient points of an elderly woman with badly dyed hair but surprisingly expensive-looking shoes and handbag, followed by a man of indeterminate age with the sagging jumper and straggly beard of someone with only three mates, who could all list FA Cup winners and Christmas number ones from the dawn of time. And then Gavin stumbled to a halt.

She looked like a waif crossed with a wolf. She wore a black leather vest zipped up to the hollow at the base of her throat. Not a hint of cleavage, but the promise of well-shaped breasts beneath. Her arms were bare. Well, technically, he supposed they were bare. The flesh was uncovered but scarcely exposed. Complicated, subtle tattoos covered her from wrist to shoulder like well-established vines over a pergola. They seemed to be derived from the complex designs of Chinese porcelain. Gavin's throat was suddenly dry, his tongue huge in his mouth.

He looked back at Charlie in a bid to stay calm. But his eyes drifted back to the woman. Her hair was thick and dark, cut short and choppy. In profile, her features were well-defined. He recoiled from the word 'chiselled' but it kept slinking back, annoyingly irresistible. Her eyes were the blue of indigo jeans and they were fixed on Charlie. She was concentrating, that much was obvious. What was also clear was that she wasn't exactly impressed.

Gavin tried not to stare. It took a conscious effort, but he managed to focus on Charlie, at least with his eyes. Eventually, Charlie came to the end of his spiel. Gavin would have struggled to offer any kind of summary. But now apparently they were being set an assignment. Split into groups of four, provided with a handout that listed half a dozen elements of a story set-up then posed a series of questions.

'This is the starting point for a story,' Charlie said. 'It might be a short story. It might be a novel. It might be a screenplay. That's up to you. What I want you to do in your groups is to brainstorm these bullet points and questions and come up with a plotline. You've got twenty minutes to work on that before the end of class. Your assignment for next week is to take that plotline away and write your version of the first fifteen hundred words of whatever it is.' He spread his arms in a gesture of generosity. 'Enjoy yourselves.' Then he turned away and opened his iPad.

They were in the same group. Gavin didn't even have to engineer it. They fell naturally together, along with the bad-hair-dye woman and the straggly beard bloke. The woman with the tattoos and, it turned out, the black jeans and biker boots, was Natasha. When she smiled at Gavin, he'd have sworn every internal organ clenched.

It was soon clear that Natasha was the only one of them who had any sense of how narrative worked. It wasn't that she bullied them, though. She gave everyone space to talk and didn't rubbish what they had to say. But she took their feeble suggestions and somehow converted them into plot points then strung those points together, beads on a string of story. Suddenly their fragile ideas were transformed into something that made sense. When their twenty minutes was up, Gavin was almost as excited at the prospect of writing the story as he was at the presence of Natasha.

Before he could stumble out an invitation for coffee or a drink, she'd shoved her scribbling pad and pen into her backpack, shrugged into a fake fur jacket and disappeared into the night like a Gothic apparition. Shell-shocked by the evening, Gavin hurried home, possessed by alarm, afraid the story would somehow dissolve before he got back to his laptop.

But Natasha's construction was more sturdy than that. It was like having a road map laid out before him. All he had to do was follow the itinerary, fleshing it out with characters and setting, enlivening it with dialogue and lapidary turns of phrase. Gavin had never been happier with a piece of writing. He hit the fifteen-hundred-word mark and just kept going, letting the story unfold at its own pace. When he reached the end at five thousand, three hundred and twenty-seven words, it was almost four in the morning. And yet Gavin wasn't tired. He was utterly exhilarated.

Over the next six days, Gavin tried to revise what he'd written. But even though he knew the true skill of being a writer lay in the editing and rewriting, he could find almost nothing that needed to be changed. It left him uneasy, wondering whether he'd lost touch with his critical faculty. Maybe the story was as crap as all his others had been, only he couldn't see it any more.

By the time Charlie's class rolled round, Gavin

was edgy and anxious, convinced that his instant infatuation with Natasha had blunted his sensibilities beyond repair. He had to know the truth, so when Charlie asked for volunteers to read out their work to the group, Gavin jumped to his feet. He squared his shoulders, took a deep breath and began. Their silence was unnerving, but he tried not to pay attention to that. When he reached the prescribed fifteen-hundred-word mark, he looked up, taking in their reactions for the first time. His audience were still, eyes fixed on him. Charlie cleared his throat. 'There's more, right?' he said.

'About five thousand words total,' Gavin said.

'Read it,' Charlie said. A murmur of voices agreed.

'Please, Gavin,' Natasha said.

That clinched it. Amazed at the reaction, Gavin finished the story. His words seemed to hang in the air for a breathless moment, then the group broke into loud applause. 'Christ, Gavin,' Charlie said. 'You should be teaching this class, not attending it. That's the best story I've heard in ages. Thomas Butler, what a character. We need to hear more from him, that's amazing stuff.'

As the praise mounted around him, Gavin wanted to laugh out loud. Finally, he'd found his storytelling voice. He looked for Natasha, hoping for her approval. She was on the fringes of the group, but her pleasure was obvious. She raised an imaginary glass in a toast to him.

The rest of the evening was a blur. Charlie talked

about something. Then he set another assignment. But before Gavin could corner Natasha, Charlie had a hand on his shoulder. He steered him to one side. 'You need to publish that story,' Charlie said. 'Do it yourself. Don't wait for some magazine editor to pick you off the slush pile. Straight to epub, that's the way to do it – 99p a shot. Get the word out on social media. Create a buzz. I'm telling you, Gavin, Thomas Butler could be a word-of-mouth sensation. As popular as Sherlock Holmes. As many copies sold as *Fifty Shades of Grey*.'

Gavin laughed nervously. 'I think you're getting a bit carried away, Charlie.'

He shook his head. 'No. I know narrative magic when I see it. Come to my office tomorrow morning, I'll show you how to do it.'

Dazed, Gavin walked out of the lecture theatre. But the night's surprises weren't over. When he emerged into the hallway, Natasha unpeeled herself from the wall she was leaning against and fell into step beside him. 'We need to talk,' she said. 'Can I buy you a coffee?'

She led the way to the Costa Coffee concession in the foyer of the English Studies building. At this time of the evening, it was virtually deserted, most students having abandoned coffee for alcohol. 'Latte?' she asked. He nodded, torn between delight that she'd guessed and embarrassment at not being a double espresso kind of guy.

Natasha brought the hot drinks back and sat opposite him. The intensity of her stare was disconcerting.

'I've been looking for the right person for a very long time,' she said. 'I think you might be him.'

For the first time, Gavin understood that the swooning that peppered Victorian sensation novels might not be a fiction. He felt dizzy and disorientated. 'Me?' he managed to mumble.

'I think we're the two halves of a whole,' she continued, apparently oblivious to his discomfiture. 'You see, I've always had this gift for narrative. Give me half a dozen disparate elements and I can string a story together, just like that.' She snapped her fingers. 'But when I try to write them down, they suck. I can't write to save my life. I end up with flat prose filled with clichés. Cardboard characters. Dialogue that would embarrass a Dalek.' She sighed. 'You've no idea how frustrating that is.'

By now it had dawned on Gavin that Natasha was not making a declaration of love, or even lust. 'Believe me, I do,' he said. 'Me, I can write. But I'm rubbish at coming up with stories.'

'That wasn't rubbish tonight,' Natasha said. 'That was brilliant. Transcendent. Extraordinary. You held us all in your hand. That was the best story I've heard in years.'

'But it wasn't my story. It was yours.'

'Exactly. My story, your words. You think you could do that again?'

Gavin nodded. 'I think so. I've never written anything that came so easily. It just flowed. You give me the plot, I'll give you the story.' He held up a finger, putting her on hold for a moment. 'But can you make it about Thomas Butler? Charlie seems to think I can sell tonight's story online. If he's right, I should try to build up a following for the character, right?'

Natasha's smile was slow and sexy. 'Thomas Butler, steampunk detective. He's a good character, Gavin.' She stared into her coffee for a moment, eyebrows furled in thought. Then she leaned back and began. 'Two halves of a whole, Gavin. Remember that.'

It turned out Charlie had been right. It took a few months for the word to spread, but within nine months, the Thomas Butler stories had grown into a global word-of-mouth phenomenon. Millions of readers had downloaded each of the ten stories Gavin and Natasha had conjured up and posted online on the first of every month. To their delight, they were making money. Even with the fifty-fifty split they'd agreed on at the start, both were earning more than they'd ever imagined possible. Two publishing conglomerates had locked horns in an auction to win the rights to a physical version of the stories. A TV series was in production and their agent reported three companies were bidding for the film rights. It was almost too good to be true. Except that it was happening.

Gavin was bemused to find his dream had become a reality. The only downside was the constant pressure for interviews and personal appearances. He refused almost every approach, which only seemed to make people more eager. As he pointed out to Natasha, she'd be a much better subject for interviews. But nobody knew Natasha played any part in the Thomas Butler phenomenon. That was the other thing they'd agreed at the start. They'd split the money up the middle, but the credit would all be Gavin's. 'It just sounds too weird otherwise,' she'd said.

Weird or not, it worked. Not just in terms of fiction either. Creating fiction together had acted on their emotions like a supercharger. Within days of putting their heads together over Thomas Butler, they'd become lovers. Within a couple of weeks, their lives were as closely intertwined as Natasha's tattoos. Gavin could spend hours at a time lying next to her, memorising the elaborate designs that wound their way up her arms and across her torso. Everything about her was endlessly fascinating. Only an outsider anatomising their relationship might have noticed how little they talked about their past. The road that had brought them to each other was far less interesting than the one they were forging together, stretching into a joint future.

When the end came, it was sudden, swift and shocking. Late in the evening, as usual, Gavin had begun a new Thomas Butler. The only fuel he needed was the words, but Natasha needed coffee and there was none. So she'd set off on her bike for the 24-hour supermarket two kilometres away. Her bike was garishly lit. Too garishly, perhaps, one of the traffic cops dared to suggest. Such brightness was bound to catch the eye, to distract a driver long enough for him to swerve into the cycle lane. Long enough for his SUV to mash Natasha and her bike into an inseparable mess. By the time they'd identified her, Gavin had finished the latest story.

Gavin tried really hard not to fall apart. He made a point of not getting drunk. He refused to take sleeping pills or anti-depressants. He didn't open the thousands of messages of condolence from fans and friends. 'I'm not ill. I'm just sad,' he told Charlie Arthur when the novelist came round to check on his former student.

'Are you writing?' Charlie asked.

Gavin didn't know how to begin to answer that question. There was a vast jagged hole in the middle of his life. He'd lost the wellspring of love from his life and with it had gone his stories. How could he ever expect to write again? And what did it matter anyway? Without Natasha, there was no point.

The days crawled by. Like an automaton, he dealt with the nuts and bolts of the business that had grown around Thomas Butler. Some nights, Gavin managed to sleep for a few hours, but mostly he walked by the river, numb and cold. He'd lost all sense of the passage of time. He didn't even notice that the month was drawing to a close. All around the world, Thomas Butler fans were waiting with bated breath to see whether Gavin's grief meant they'd be cut off from their drug of choice.

On the last night of the month, Gavin went to bed with no expectation of sleep. He lay curled on his side in the dark, the soft hum of the city for his night music. And then it happened. It started at his feet. A deep chill spread through his toes and up to his ankles. Then the back of his calves. The cold rose through the back of his body, ending at the nape of his neck. Then a band of ice crossed his arm and settled on his chest. The chill seemed to penetrate his body, making it impossible to move. Bewildered, Gavin could make no sense of what was happening. It was like an embrace in reverse. Instead of being warmed by a lover's body, it was as if a wintry presence was sucking the warmth from him. His heart raced in panic but curiously, the only coherent thought in his head was that when Natasha came to bed late and cold, this was momentarily how it felt. Cold feet against his, then the press of her chilly body and her arm across his chest. But that cold only ever lasted for moments. It didn't cut through to his bones. And besides, Natasha was gone.

Except she wasn't. He could hear her in his head as clearly as if she was in the room with him. 'I miss you, Gavin,' she said, her voice cracking on his name.

He tried to tell her how much he missed her, how his chest hurt all the time, how his throat was always full of tears. But speech was beyond him. His mouth wouldn't work.

'I've come to tell you a story,' Natasha said. 'I know you can't do it without me, so I've come back. Listen carefully. This is how it begins.'

Her words poured into his head, weaving their inevitable, irresistible tale. At last, she said, 'The End.' And without warning, she was gone. Warmth returned to Gavin's body and he was wide awake, a story banging at the doors of his mind.

Gingerly he got up and went to his laptop, almost afraid to lay his fingers on the keyboard. He felt as if he was standing outside himself, watching the words form on the screen from a distance. Whatever was happening, it was beyond his control. The sentences piled up in front of his eyes and as he understood that a story was growing, he felt his grief ease for the first time since Natasha's death.

He finished the story as the sky was lightening and posted it online. Then he went back to bed, comforted beyond words by the thought that Natasha had not left him completely.

And so it continued for the next eight months. On the last night of every month, Gavin would go to bed and the chill ghost of his lover would embrace him, revealing a fresh plot for him to translate into a rich and engaging narrative. He learned quickly not to question the gift. At first, he'd tried to convince himself it was a delusion. That somehow, he'd finally learned from Natasha how to tell a story. But every time he sat down and tried to create his own story, he could only make something as pitiful as his old solo efforts. Whatever was happening here, it was happening because of her. Not because of him. And it healed him better than any therapy could have done.

The world outside moved on, of course. The Thomas

Butler frenzy showed no sign of abating. Gavin had a literary agent now, who protected him from most of the craziness, but there were some occasions he couldn't escape. Some even appealed to him. The TV company who were adapting the Thomas Butler stories invited him to meet the production designer and the composer, and Gavin thought that might be bearable.

Ella Garrison, the composer, was the first woman he'd met since Natasha who intrigued him. Music absorbed her, that much was clear. And the sketches she played him for the Thomas Butler adaptation moved him in a way he'd thought was beyond him these days. The lunch where they'd been introduced spread into the evening, and they parted with a promise to meet again soon.

Within days they were in constant communication – texting, messaging, sharing music and books. The unexpectedness of it left Gavin reeling. But Natasha's visitations had convinced him that she would give these fresh green shoots of recovery her blessing. What else could her gifts of story mean if not that his life should go on? And so he handed himself over to the unforeseen.

But on the last night of the month, he left Ella's bed and went home. A new story was due in the morning, after all, and it seemed tacky to be in bed with one woman while accepting gifts from another. Gavin slipped under the duvet and gradually drifted away into what he considered his receptive state.

And woke seven hours later without an idea in his head.

He couldn't quite believe it. He went to the laptop and put his fingers on the keys. Nothing. Utter blank emptiness. What the hell was this? Surely Natasha didn't mean him to live like a monk for the rest of his life, devoted to her memory and the creation of Thomas Butler? How could she be so unreasonable?

Gavin paced the floor, anxious and angry. It wasn't as if he could share his dilemma with anyone else; nobody knew about the original arrangement with Natasha, not really, not the details. And nobody would believe her spirit had been visiting him with the gift of stories. And meanwhile, his phone buzzed with urgent messages from his agent and everybody else who had a vested interest in the new Thomas Butler story which had not appeared on the website that morning.

Finally, worn out with emotion and pacing, he threw himself down on the sofa and fell asleep. And then it happened. The chill, the paralysis, the voice in his head. And when he woke, there was a story, perfectly formed, ready to be fleshed out. Gavin almost wept with relief as his fingers tapped out the latest instalment of Thomas Butler's steampunk existence. Whatever Natasha was playing at, she'd got over herself and delivered. And thank God for that. The thought of the world discovering that he was not the genius who had given them Thomas Butler made Gavin feel positively nauseous. He had a reputation now, not to mention an income. He couldn't bear the thought of losing either of those. Never mind the gift of being able to put his skills to good service.

After that one hiccup, however, paranormal service was resumed. For the next two months, Natasha appeared on deadline night, weaving the kind of stories Gavin had become famous for. As he grew closer to Ella, he felt a secure sense of a future. Three stories now since they'd got together; nothing had changed in his professional life after all.

A different kind of story broke four days after Gavin uploaded that third tale to the website. According to a reliable media source, the three latest Thomas Butler stories had been plagiarised from the work of three obscure Chinese writers. Writers whose work had never been translated from their native language. Writers whose work appeared in chapbooks that had been checked out of the university library over the past year by Chinese translator Gavin Blake. Writers who were now preparing killer lawsuits against Gavin and his publishers.

Gavin read the reports with a growing sense of horror. As he read, a chill enveloped the back of his head, an icy hand ruffling his hair. 'It's not as if I didn't warn you,' Natasha said. 'Two halves of a whole, remember?'

WHITE
NIGHTS,
BLACK
MAGIC

When night falls in St Petersburg, the dead become more palpable. In this city built on blood and bone, they're always present. But when darkness gathers, they're harder to escape. The frozen, drowned serfs who paid the price for Peter the Great's determination to fulfil Nostradamus's prediction that Venice would rise from the dead waters of the north; the assassinated tsars whose murders changed surprisingly little; the starved victims of the Wehrmacht's nine-hundred-day siege; the buried corpses of lords of the imagination such as Dostoevsky, Borodin and Rimsky-Korsakov – they're all there in the shifting shadows, their foetid breath tainting the chilly air that comes off the Neva and shivers through the streets.

My dead too. I never feel closer to Elinor than when I walk along the embankment of Vasilyevsky Ostrov on a winter's night. The familiar grandeur of the Hermitage and St Isaac's cathedral on the opposite bank touch me not at all. What resonates inside me is the sound of her voice, the touch of her hand, the spark of her eyes.

It shouldn't be this way. It shouldn't be the darkness that conjures her up for me, because we didn't make those memories in the dead core of winter. The love that exploded between us was a child of the light, a dream state that played itself out against the backdrop of the White Nights, those heady summer weeks when the sun never sets over St Petersburg.

Like all lovers, we thought the sun would never set on us either. But it did. And although Elinor isn't one of the St Petersburg dead, she comes back to haunt me when the city's ghosts drift through the streets in wraiths of river mist. I know too that this is no neutral visitation. Her presence demands something of me, and it's taken me a long time to figure out what that is. But I know now. Elinor understood that Russia can be a cruel and terrible place, and also that I am profoundly Russian. So tonight, I will make reparation.

Three summers ago, Elinor unpacked her bags in the Moscow Hotel down at the far end of Nevsky Prospekt. She'd never been to Russia before, and when we met that first evening, she radiated a buzz of excitement that enchanted me. We Russians are bound to our native land by a terrible, doomed sentimental attachment, and we are predisposed to like anyone who shows the slightest sign of sharing that love.

But there was more than that linking us from the very beginning. Anyone who has ever been in an abusive relationship has had their mental map altered forever. It's hard to explain precisely how that manifests itself, but once you've been there, you recognise it in another. An almost imperceptible flicker in the eyes; some tiny shift in the body language; an odd moment of deference in the dialogue. Whatever the signals, they're subconsciously registered by those of us who are members of the same club. In that very first encounter, I read that kinship between myself and Elinor.

By the time I met Elinor, I was well clear of the marriage that had thrown me off balance, turned me from a confident, assured professional woman into a bundle of insecurities. I was back on an even keel, in control of my own destiny and certain I would never walk into that nightmare again. I wasn't so sure about Elinor.

She seemed poised and assertive. She was a well-qualified doctor who had gained a reputation for her work on addiction with intravenous drug users in her native Manchester. She was the obvious choice for a month-long exchange visit to share her experiences with local medical professionals and voluntary-sector workers struggling to come to terms with the heroin epidemic sweeping St Petersburg. She exuded a quiet competence and easy manner. But still, I recognised the secret shame, the hidden scars.

I had been chosen to act as her interpreter because I'd spent two years of my post-graduate medical training in San Francisco. I was nervous about the assignment because I had no formal training in interpreting, but my boss made it clear there was no room for argument. The budget wouldn't run to a qualified interpreter, and besides, I knew all the technical terminology. I explained this to Elinor over a glass of wine in the half-empty bar after the official dinner with the meeting-and-greeting party.

Some specialists might have regarded my confession as a slight on their importance. But Elinor just grinned and said, 'Natasha, you're a doctor, you can probably make me sound much more sensible than I can manage myself. Now, if you're not rushing off, maybe you can show me round a little, help me get my bearings?'

We walked out of the hotel, round the corner to the Metro station. Her eyes were wide, absorbed by everything. The amputee war veterans round the kiosks; the endless escalator; the young woman slumped against the door of the train carriage, vodka bottle dangling from her fingers, wrecked mascara in snail trails down her cheeks; Elinor drank it all in, tossing occasional questions at me.

We emerged back into daylight at the opposite end of Nevsky Prospekt, and I steered her round the big tourist sights. The cathedral, the Admiralty, the Hermitage, then back along the embankment to the Fontanka Canal. Because she was still operating on UK time, she didn't really register the White Nights phenomenon at first. It was only when I pointed out that it was already eleven o'clock and she probably needed to think about getting some sleep that she realised her normal cues for waking and sleeping were going to be absent for the next four weeks.

'How do you cope with the constant light?' she said, waving an arm at a sky only a couple of shades lighter than her eyes.

I shrugged. 'I pull the pillow over my head. But your hotel will have heavy curtains, I think.' I flagged down a passing Lada and asked the driver to take us back to the hotel.

'It's all so alien,' she said softly.

'It'll get worse before it gets better,' I told her. I dropped her at the hotel and kept the car on. As the driver weaved through the potholed streets back to my apartment on Vasilyevsky Ostrov, I couldn't escape the image of her wide-eyed wondering face.

But then, I wasn't exactly trying.

Over the next week, I spent most of my waking hours with Elinor. Mostly it was work, constantly stretching my brain to keep pace with the exchange of information that flowed back and forth between Elinor and my colleagues. But in the evenings, we fell into the habit of eating together, then strolling around the city so she could soak up the atmosphere. I didn't mind. There were plenty of other things I could have been doing, but my friends would still be there after she left town. What I wasn't allowing myself to acknowledge was that I was falling in love with her.

On the sixth night, she finally started opening up. 'You know I mentioned my partner?' she said, filling our wine glasses to avoid my eyes.

'He's a lawyer, right?' I said.

Her mouth twisted up at one corner. 'He's a she.' She flicked a quick glance at me. 'Does that surprise you?'

I couldn't keep the smile from my face. For days,

I'd been telling myself off for wishful thinking, but I'd been right. 'It takes one to know one,' I said.

'You're gay?' Elinor sounded startled.

'Labels are for medicines,' I said. 'But lately, I seem to have given up on men.'

'You have a girlfriend?' Now, her eyes were on mine. I didn't know what to read into their level stare, which unsettled me a little.

'Nothing serious,' I said. 'A friend I sleep with from time to time, when she's in town. Just fun, for both of us. Not like you.'

She looked away again. 'No. Not like me.'

Something about the angle of her head, the down-cast eyes and the hand that gripped the wine glass told me my first instinct had been right. Whatever she might say next, I knew that this apparently confident woman was in thrall to someone who stripped her of her self-esteem. 'Tell me about her,' I said.

'Her name's Claire. She's a lawyer, specialising in intellectual property. She's very good. We've been together ten years. She's very smart, very strong, very beautiful. She keeps my feet on the ground.'

I wanted to tell her that love should be about flying, not about the force of gravity. But I didn't. 'Do you miss her?'

Again, she met my eyes. 'I thought I would. But I've been so busy.' She smiled. 'And you're such good company, you've kept me from being lonely.'

'It's been my pleasure. Where would you like to go this evening?'

Her gaze was level, unblinking. 'I'd like to see where you live.'

I tried to stay cool. 'It's not very impressive.'

'You don't have to impress me. I'd just like to see a real Russian home. I'm fed up with hotels and restaurants.'

So we took the Metro to Vasileostrovskaya and walked down Sredny Prospekt to the Tenth Line, where I live in a two-roomed apartment on the second floor. Buying it took every penny I managed to save in the US, and it's pretty drab by Western standards, but to a Russian it feels like total luxury to have so much space to oneself. I showed Elinor into the living room with some nervousness. I'd never brought a Westerner home before.

She looked around the white walls with their Chagall posters and the second-hand furniture covered with patchwork throws, then turned to me and smiled. 'I like it,' she said.

I turned away, feeling embarrassed. 'Interior design hasn't really hit Russia,' I said. 'Would you like a drink? I've got tea or coffee or vodka.'

'Vodka, please.'

There is a moment that comes with drinking vodka Russian style when inhibitions slip away. That's the time to stop drinking, before you get too drunk to do anything with the window of opportunity. I knew Elinor had hit the moment when she leaned into me and said, 'I really love this country.'

I pushed her dark hair from her forehead and said,

'Russia can be a very cruel place. We Russians are dangerous.'

'You don't feel very dangerous to me,' she whispered, her breath hot against my neck.

'I'm Russian. I'm trouble. The two go together like hand in glove.'

'Mmm. I like the sound of that. Your hand, my glove.'

'That would be very dangerous.'

She chuckled softly. 'I feel the need for a little danger, Natasha.'

And so we made trouble.

Of course, she went back to England. She didn't want to, but she had no choice. Her visa was about to expire, she had work commitments at home. And there was Claire. She had said very little about her lover, but I understood how deeply ingrained was her subservience. The clues were there, both sexually and emotionally. Claire wasn't physically violent, but emotional abuse can cause damage that is far more profound. Elinor had learned the lesson of submission so thoroughly it was entrenched in her soul. No matter how deep the love that had sprung up between us, in her heart she couldn't escape the conviction that she belonged to Claire.

It didn't stop us loving each other. We emailed daily, sometimes several times a day. We managed to speak on the phone every two or three weeks, sometimes for an hour at a time. A couple of months after she'd gone back, she called in distress. Claire had accepted a new job in London, and was insisting Elinor abandon her work in Manchester and move to the capital with her. I gently suggested this might be the opportunity for Elinor to free herself, not necessarily for me but for her own sake. But I knew even as I spoke it was pointless. Until Claire decided it was over, Elinor had no other option but to stay. I understood that; I had only managed to free myself when my husband had grown tired of me. I wanted to save her, but I didn't know how.

Three months later, they'd moved. Elinor had found a job at one of the London teaching hospitals. She didn't have the same degree of autonomy she'd enjoyed in Manchester, and she found it much less challenging. But at least she was able to use some of her expertise, and she liked the team she was working with.

I was actually reading one of her emails when my boss called me into his office. 'You know I'm supposed to go to London next week? The conference on HIV and intravenous drug use?'

I nodded. Lucky bastard, I'd thought when the invitation came through. 'I remember.'

'My wife has been diagnosed with breast cancer,' he said abruptly. 'They're operating on Monday. So you'll have to go instead.'

It was an uncomfortable way to achieve my heart's desire, but there was nothing I could do about my boss's misfortune. A few days later, I was walking through customs and immigration and into Elinor's arms. We went straight to my hotel and dived back into the dangerous waters. Hand in glove. Moths to a flame.

Four days of the conference. Three evenings supposedly socialising with colleagues, but in reality, time we could steal to be together. Except that on the last night, the plans went spectacularly awry. Instead of a discreet knock at my bedroom door, the phone rang. Elinor's voice was unnaturally bright. 'Hi Natasha,' she said. 'I'm down in reception. I hope you don't mind, but I've brought Claire with me. She wanted to meet you.'

Panic choked me like a gloved hand. 'I'll be right down,' I managed to say. I dressed hurriedly, fingers fumbling zip and buttons, mouth muttering Russian curses. What was Claire up to? Was this simply about control, or was there more to it? Had she sussed what was going on between Elinor and me? With dry mouth and damp palms, I rode the lift to the ground floor, trying to hold it together. Not for myself, but for Elinor's sake.

They looked good together. Elinor's sable hair, denim-blue eyes and olive skin on one side of the table, a contrast to Claire's blonde hair and surprising brown eyes. Where Elinor's features where small and neat, Claire's were strong and well-defined. She looked like someone you'd rather have on your side than against you. While Elinor looked nervous, her fingers picking at a cocktail coaster, Claire leaned back in her seat, a woman in command of her surroundings.

As I approached, feeling hopelessly provincial next to their urban chic, Claire was first to her feet. 'You must be Natasha,' she said, her smile lighting her eyes. 'I'm so pleased to meet you.' I extended a hand, but her hand was on my shoulder as she leaned in to kiss me on both cheeks. 'I've been telling Elinor off for keeping you to herself. I do hope you don't mind me butting in, but I so wanted to meet you.'

Control, then, I thought, daring to let myself feel relieved as I sat down at the table. At once, Claire stamped her authority on the conversation. How was I enjoying London? Was it as I expected? How were things in Russia? How was life changing for ordinary people?

By the time we hit the second drink, she was flirting with me. She wanted to prove she could own me the way she owned her lover. Elinor was consigned to the sidelines, and her acquiescence to this confirmed all I believed about their relationship. My heart ached for her, an uneasy mixture of love and pity making me feel faintly queasy. I don't know how I managed to eat dinner with them. All I wanted was to steal Elinor away, to prove to her that she had the power to take her life back and make of it what she wanted.

But of course, she left with Claire. And in the morning, I was on a plane back to St Petersburg, half-convinced that the only healthy thing for me to do was to end our relationship.

I didn't. I couldn't. In spite of everything I know about the tentacles of emotional abuse, I found it impossible to reject the notion that I might somehow be Elinor's saviour. So I kept on writing, kept on telling her how much I loved her when she called, kept on seeing her face in my mind's eye whenever I slept with other people.

More weeks trickled by, then out of the blue, an email in a very different tone arrived.

Natasha, darling. Can you get to Brussels next weekend? I need to see you. I can arrange air tickets if you can arrange a visa. Please, if it's humanly possible, come to Brussels.

I love you.

E.

I tried to get her to tell me what was going on, but she refused. All I could do was fix up a visa and collect the tickets from the travel agent. When Elinor opened the hotel room door, she looked a dozen years older than when I'd seen her in London. My first thought was that Claire had discovered our affair. But the truth was infinitely worse.

We'd barely hugged when Elinor was moving away from me. She curled up in the room's only armchair and covered her face with her hands. 'I'm so scared,' she said.

I crouched down beside her and gently pulled her hands away from her face. 'What's wrong, Elinor?'

She flicked her tongue along dry lips. 'You know I'm mostly working with HIV patients now?'

It wasn't what I'd expected to hear, but somehow I already knew what was coming. 'Yes, I know.'

A deep, shuddering breath. 'A few weeks ago, I got a needle stick.' Her eyes filled with tears. 'Natasha, I'm HIV positive.'

Intellectually, I knew this wasn't a death sentence. So did Elinor. But in that instant, it felt like the end of the world. I couldn't think of anything else that would assert her right to a future, so I cradled her in my arms and said, 'Let's make love.'

At first, she resisted. But we both knew too much about the transmission routes of the virus for the idea of putting me at risk to take deep root. Sure, it meant changes for how we made love, but that was a tiny price to pay for the affirmation that her life would go on.

We spent the weekend behind closed doors, loving each other, talking endlessly about what she'd have to do to maximise her chances of long-term health. At some point on Sunday, she confessed that Claire had refused to have sex since the diagnosis. That made me angrier than anything I'd previously known or suspected about the abuse of power between the two of them.

That parting was the worst. I wanted to take her home with me. I wanted our passion to be a cocoon against the virus. But realistically, even if she'd been able to leave Claire, we both knew her best chance for access to the latest treatments would be to remain in the West.

Oddly, in spite of the cataclysmic nature of her news, nothing really changed between us. The old channels of communication remained intact, the intensity between us diminished not at all. The only difference was that now we also discussed drug treatments, dietary regimes and alternative therapies.

Then one Monday, silence. No email. I wasn't too worried. There had been days when Elinor hadn't been able to write, but mostly those had been on the weekend when she'd not been able to escape Claire's oppressive attention. Tuesday dragged past, then Wednesday. No reply to my emails, no phone call. Nothing. Finally, on the Thursday, I tried to call her at work.

Voicemail. I left an innocuous message and hung up. Friday brought more silence. The weekend was a nightmare. I checked my email neurotically, every hour, on the hour. I was afraid to go out in case she called, and by Sunday night my apartment felt like a prison cell. Monday, I spoke to her voicemail again. Desperation had me in its grip. I even considered taking the chance of calling her at home. Instead, I hit on the idea of calling the department secretary.

'I've been trying to contact Dr Stevenson,' I said when I finally got through.

'Dr Stevenson is away at present,' the stiff English voice said.

'When will she be back?'

'I really can't say.'

I'd been fighting fear for days, but now my defences were crumbling fast. 'Look, I'm a personal friend of Elinor's,' I said. 'From St Petersburg. I'm due to be in

London this week and we were supposed to meet. But I've had no reply to my emails, and I really need to contact her about our arrangements. Can you help me?'

The voice softened. 'I'm afraid Dr Stevenson's very ill. She won't be well enough to have a meeting this week.'

'Is she in hospital?' Somehow, I managed to keep hold of my English in the teeth of the terror that was ripping through me.

'Yes, she's a patient here.'

'Can you put me through to the ward she's on?'

'I'm ... I'm sorry, she's in intensive care. She won't be able to speak to you.'

I don't remember ending the call. Just the desperate pain her words brought in their wake. I couldn't make sense of what I was hearing. It ran counter to all I knew about HIV and AIDS. It was a matter of months since Elinor had been infected. For her to be so ill so soon was virtually unheard of. People lived with HIV for years. Some people lived with AIDS for years. It was impossible.

But the impossible had happened.

I spent the next couple of days in a frenzy of activity, staving off my alarm with action. I couldn't afford the flight, but I managed to get the money together by borrowing from my three closest friends. I couldn't even explain to my boss why I needed the time off and we were under pressure at work, so there was no prospect of making it to London before the weekend. The rest of my spare time I spent trying to sort out a visa.

By Thursday evening, I was almost organised. The travel agent had sworn she would call first thing in the morning about last-minute flights. I'd managed to persuade a colleague to cover for me at the beginning of the following week so I had a couple of extra days in hand. And the visa was promised for the next afternoon.

I'd just walked through the door of my apartment when the phone rang. I ran across the room and grabbed it. '*Da?*'

Breathing rasped in my ear. 'Natasha.' Elinor's voice was little more than a whisper but there was no mistaking it.

'Elinor.' I couldn't speak through the lump in my throat.

'I'm dying, Nat. Pneumocystis. Drug-resistant strain.' She could only speak on the exhalation of her shallow breaths. 'Wanted to call you. Brain's fucked, couldn't remember the number. Claire wouldn't ... bring me my organiser. Had to get nurse to get it from my office.'

'Never mind. We're talking now. Elinor, I'm coming over. At the weekend.'

'No. Don't come, Nat. Please. I love you too much. Don't want you to remember ... this. Remember the good stuff.'

'I want to see you.' Tears running down my face, I struggled to keep them out of my voice.

'Please, no. Nat, I wanted you to know ... loving you? Best thing that ever hit me. Wanted to say good-bye. Wanted to say, be happy.'

'*Ya tebya lublu*,' I gulped. 'Don't die on me, Elinor.'

'Wish I had ... choice. Trouble with being a doctor ... you know what's happening to you. A couple of days, Nat. Then it's ... DNR time. I love you.'

'I know.'

The breathing stopped and another voice came on the line. 'Hello? I'm sorry, Dr Stevenson is too tired to talk any more.'

'How bad is it?' I don't know how I managed to speak without choking.

'I shouldn't really speak to anyone who isn't imme-diate family,' she hedged.

'Please. You saw how important this call was to her. I'm a doctor too, I know the score.'

'I'm afraid her condition is very serious. She's not responding to treatment. It's likely we'll have to put her on a ventilator very soon.'

'Is it true she's signed a DNR?'

'I'm very sorry,' the nurse said after a short pause.

'Take good care of her.' I replaced the phone as gently as if it had been Elinor's hand. I'd spent enough time in hospital to read between the lines. Elinor hadn't been mistaken. She was dying.

I never went to London. It would have been an act of selfishness. Claire never called me, which told me that she knew the truth. But the nurse from intensive care did phone, on the Sunday morning at nine twenty-seven a.m. Elinor had asked her to let me know when she died.

A couple of weeks later, I wrote to Claire, saying I'd heard about Elinor's death from a colleague and expressing my sympathy. I'm not sure why I did, but sometimes our subconscious paves the way for our future actions without bothering to inform us.

Grief twisted in me like a rusty knife for a long time. But everything transmutes eventually, and slowly it turned to anger. Generally when people die, there's nobody to blame. But Elinor's death wasn't like that. The responsibility for what happened to her lay with Claire, impossible to dodge.

If Claire had not ruled her with fear, Elinor would have left her for me. If Claire had not stripped her of her self-confidence, Elinor would have stayed in Manchester and someone else would have suffered that needle stick. However you cut it, Elinor would still be alive if Claire had not made her feel like a possession.

For a long time my anger felt pointless, a dry fire burning inside me that consumed nothing. Then out of the blue, I had an email from Claire.

Hello, Natasha.

I'm sorry I never got in touch with you after Elinor's death, but as you will imagine, it was not an easy time for me. However, I am attending a conference in St Petersburg next month, and I wondered if you would like to meet up for dinner. I have such fond memories of the evening we spent together in London. It might bring us both some solace to spend some time together. Let me know if this would suit you.

Best wishes, Claire Somerville.

The arrangements are made. Tonight, she will come to my apartment for dinner. I know she will seduce me. She won't be able to resist the challenge of possessing the woman Elinor loved.

But Claire is a Russian virgin. She doesn't understand the first thing about us. She will have no sense of the cruelty or the danger that always lurks beneath the surface, particularly in this city of the dead.

She will not suspect the narcotic in the alcohol. And when she wakes, she won't notice the scab on the vein in the back of her knee. The syringe is loaded already, thick with virus, carefully maintained in perfect culture conditions.

It's almost certain she'll have longer than Elinor. But sooner or later, the black magic of those White Nights will take its revenge. And perhaps then, my dead will sleep.

HEARTBURN

Everybody remarked on how calm I was on Bonfire Night. 'Considering her husband's just run off with another woman, she's very calm,' I overheard Joan Winstanley from the newsagent's say as I persuaded people to buy the bonfire toffee. But it seemed to me that Derek's departure was no reason to miss the annual cricket-club fireworks party. Besides, I've been in charge of the toffee-selling now for more years than I care to remember, and I'd be reluctant to hand it over to someone else.

So I put a brave face on it and turned up as usual at Mrs Fletcher's at half past five to pick up the toffee, neatly bagged up in quarter-pound lots. I don't know how she does it, given that the pieces are all such irregular shapes and sizes, but the bags all contain the correct weight. I know, because the second year I was in charge of the toffee, I surreptitiously took the bags home and weighed them. I wasn't prepared to be responsible for selling short weight.

Of course, the jungle drums had been beating. Oswaldtwistle is a small town, after all. Strange to think that's what drew Derek and me here all those years ago, willing refugees from the inner-city problems of Manchester. Anyway, Mrs Fletcher greeted me with, 'I hear he's gone off.'

Shamefaced, I nodded. 'He did finish building the bonfire before he left,' I added timidly.

'She's always been no better than she should be, that Janice Duckworth. Of course, your Derek's not the first she's led astray. Though she's never actually gone off with any of them before. That does surprise me. Always liked having her cake and eating it, has Janice.'

I tried to ignore Mrs Fletcher's remarks, but they burned inside me like the scarlet and yellow flames of the makeshift bonfire I'd already passed on the churned-up mud of the rec at the end of her street. I grabbed the toffee ungraciously, and got out as soon as I could.

I drove through the narrow terraced streets rather too fast, something I'm not particularly given to. All around me, the crump and flash of fireworks gave a shocking life to the evening. Rocket trails show-ered their sparks across the sky like a sudden rash of comets, all predicting the end of the world. Except that the end of my world had come the night before.

Constructing the bonfire had always taken a lot of Derek's time in the weeks leading up to the cricket-club fireworks party. As a civil engineer, he prided himself on its elaborate design and execution. The secret, he told me so often I could recite it from memory, the secret is to build from the middle outwards.

To achieve the perfect bonfire, according to Derek, it was necessary first to construct what looked like a little hut at the heart of the fire. Derek usually made this from planks the thickness of floorboards. The first couple of years I accompanied him, so I speak from the experience of having seen it as well as having heard the lecture on countless occasions. To me, Derek's central structure looked like nothing so much as a primitive outside lavatory.

Round the 'hut', Derek would then build an elaborate construction of wood, cardboard, chipboard, old furniture and anything else that seemed combustible. But the key to his success was that he left a tunnel through the shell of the bonfire that led to the hut.

The night before the bonfire was lit, late in the evening, after all the local hooligans could reasonably be expected to be abed, Derek would enter the tunnel, crawl to the heart of his construction and fill the hut with a mixture of old newspapers and petrol-soaked rags in plastic bags.

Then he would crawl out, back-filling the tunnel behind him with more highly flammable materials. The point at which the tunnel ended, on the perimeter of the bonfire, was where it had to be lit for maximum effect, burning high and bright for hours.

There are doubtless those who think it highly irresponsible to leave the bonfire in so vulnerable a condition overnight, but the cricket club is pretty secure, with a high fence that no one would dream of trying to scale, since it's overlooked by the police station. Besides, because the bonfire was the responsibility of adults, it never became a target for the kind of childish gang rivalry that leads to bonfires being set alight in advance of the scheduled event.

Anyway, this year as usual, Derek went off the night before the fireworks party to put the finishing touches to his monument, carrying the flask of hot coffee laced with brandy which I always provided to help combat the raw November weather. When he hadn't come home by midnight, naturally I was concerned. My first thought was that he'd had some sort of problem with the bonfire. Perhaps a heavy piece of wood had fallen on him, pinning him to the ground. I drove down to the cricket ground, but it was deserted. The bonfire was finished, though. I checked.

I went home and paced the floor for a while, then I rang the police. Sergeant Mills was very sympathetic, understanding that Derek was not a man to stay out till the small hours except when attending one of those masculine events that involve consuming huge amounts of alcohol and telling the sort of stories we women are supposed to be too sensitive to hear. If he'd been invited back to a fellow member of the fireworks party committee's home for a nightcap, he would have rung to let me know. He knows how I worry if he's more than a few minutes later than he's told me he'd be. But of course, there was nothing the police could do. Derek is a grown man, after all, and the law allows grown men to stay out all night, if they so desire.

I called Sergeant Mills again the following morning, explaining that there seemed to be no reason to worry, at least not for the police, since, on searching Derek's office for clues, I had uncovered several notes from Janice Duckworth, indicating that they were having an affair and that she wanted them to run away together. It appeared that Derek had been using the bonfire-building as an excuse for seeing more of Janice. I had rung Janice's home, and ascertained from her husband Vic that she too had not returned home from an evening out, supposedly with the girls.

The case seemed cut and dried, as far as Sergeant Mills was concerned. It was humiliating and galling for me, of course, but these things do happen, especially, the sergeant seemed to hint, where middle-aged men and younger blondes are concerned.

I sold out more quickly than usual this year. I suspect the nosey parkers were seeking me out 'to see how I was taking it' rather than waiting for me to come round to them. Seven o'clock rolled round, and the bonfire was duly lit. It was a particularly spectacular effort this year. Though I grudge admitting it, no one built a bonfire quite like Derek.

I don't suppose he thought when he was building this year's that it would be a funeral pyre for him and Janice Duckworth. He really should have thought of somewhere more romantic for their assignations than a makeshift wooden hut in the middle of a bonfire.

FOUR
CALLING
BIRDS

Noreen

You want to know who to blame for what happened last Wednesday night down at the Roxette? Margaret Thatcher, that's who. Never mind the ones that actually did it. If the finger points at anybody, it should point straight at the Iron Lady. Even though her own body's turned against her now and silenced her, nobody should let pity stand in the way of holding her to account. She made whole communities despair, and when the weak are desperate, sometimes crime seems the easiest way out. Our Dickson says that's an argument that would never stand up in a court of law. But given how useless the police round here are, it's not likely to come to that.

You want to know why what happened last Wednesday night at the Roxette happened at all? You have to go back twenty years. To the miners' strike. They teach it to the bairns now as history, but I lived through it and it's as sharp in my memory as yesterday. After she beat the Argies in the Falklands, Thatcher fell in love with the taste of victory, and the miners were her number-one target. She was determined to break us, and she didn't care what it took. Arthur Scargill, the miners' leader, was as bloody-minded as she was, and when he called his men out on strike, my Alan walked out along with every other miner in his pit.

We all thought it would be over in a matter of weeks at the most. But no bugger would give an inch. Weeks turned into months, the seasons slipped from spring through summer and autumn into winter. We had four bairns to feed and not a penny coming in. Our savings went; then our insurance policies; and finally, my jewellery. We'd go to bed hungry and wake up the same way, our bellies rumbling like the slow grumble of the armoured police vans that regularly rolled round the streets of our town to remind us who we were fighting. Sometimes they'd taunt us by sitting in their vans flaunting their takeaways, even throwing half-eaten fish suppers out on the pavements as they drove by. Anything to rub our noses in the overtime they were coining by keeping us in our places.

We were desperate. I heard tell that some of the wives even went on the game, taking a bus down to the big cities for the day. But nobody from round our way sank that low. Or not that I know of. But lives changed forever during that long hellish year, mine among them.

It's a measure of how low we all sank that when I heard Mattie Barnard had taken a heart attack and died, my first thought wasn't for his widow. It was for his job. I think I got down to the Roxette faster than the Co-op Funeral Service got to Mattie's. Tyson Herbert, the manager, hadn't even heard the news.

But I didn't let that stop me. 'I want Mattie's job,' I told him straight out while he was still reeling from the shock.

'Now hang on a minute, Noreen,' he said warily. He was always cautious, was Tyson Herbert. You could lose the will to live waiting for him to turn right at a junction. 'You know as well as I do that bingo calling is a man's job. It's always been that way. A touch of authority. Dickie bow and dinner jacket. The BBC might have let their standards slip, but here at the Roxette, we do things the right way.' Ponderous as a bloody elephant.

'That's against the law nowadays, Tyson,' I said. 'You cannot have rules like that any more. Only if you're a lavatory cleaner or something. And as far as I'm aware, cleaning the gents wasn't part of Mattie's job.'

Well, we had a bit of a to and fro, but in the end, Tyson Herbert gave in. He didn't have a lot of choice. The first session of the day was due to start in half an hour, and he needed somebody up there doing two fat ladies and Maggie's den. Even if the person in question was wearing a blue nylon overall instead of a tuxedo.

And that was the start of it all. Now, nobody's ever accused me of being greedy, and besides, I still had a house to run as well as doing my share on the picket line with the other miners' wives. So within a couple of weeks, I'd persuaded Tyson Herbert that he needed to move with the times and make mine a jobshare. By the end of the month, I was splitting my shifts with Kathy, Liz and Jackie. The four calling birds, my Alan christened us. Morning, afternoon and evening, one or other of us would be up on the stage, mike in one hand, plucking balls out of the air with the other and keeping the flow of patter going. More importantly, we kept our four families going. We kept our kids on the straight and narrow.

It made a bit of a splash locally. There had never been women bingo callers in the North-East before. It had been as much a man's job as cutting coal. The local paper wrote an article about us, then the BBC turned up and did an interview with us for *Woman's Hour*. I suppose they were desperate for a story from up our way that wasn't all doom, gloom and picket lines. You should have seen Tyson Herbert preening himself, like he'd single-handedly burned every bra in the North-East.

The fuss soon died down, though the novelty value did bring in a lot of business. Women would come in minibuses from all around the area just to see the four calling birds. And we carried on with two little ducks and the key to the door like it was second nature. The years trickled past. The bairns grew up and found jobs, which was hard on Alan's pride. He's never worked since they closed the pit the year after the strike. There's no words for what it does to a man when he's dependent on his wife and bairns for the roof over his head and the food on his table.

To tell you the God's honest truth, there were days when it was a relief to get down to the Roxette and get to work. We always had a laugh, even in the hardest of times. And there were hard times. When the doctors told Kathy the lump in her breast was going to kill her, we all felt the blow. But when she got too ill to work, we offered her shifts to her Julie. Tyson Herbert made some crack about hereditary peerages, but I told him to keep his nose out and count the takings.

All in all, nobody had any reason for complaint. That is, until Tyson Herbert decided it was time to retire. The bosses at head office didn't consult us about his replacement. Come to that, they didn't consult Tyson either. If they had, we'd never have ended up with Keith Corbett. Keith Cobra as Julie rechristened him two days into his reign at the Roxette after he tried to grope her at the end of her evening shift. The nickname suited him. He was a poisonous reptile.

He even looked like a snake, with his narrow wedge of a face and his little dark eyes glittering. When his tongue flicked out to lick his thin lips, you expected it to have a fork at the end. On the third morning, he summoned the four of us to his office like he was God and it was Judgement Day. 'You've had a good run, ladies,' he began, without so much as a cup of tea and a digestive biscuit. 'But things are going to be changing round here. The Roxette is going to be the premier bingo outlet in the area, and that will be reflected in our public image. I'm giving you a formal notice of redundancy.'

We were gobsmacked. It was Liz who found her voice first. 'You cannot do that,' she said. 'We've given no grounds for complaint.'

'And how can we be redundant?' I chipped in. 'Somebody has to call the numbers.'

Cobra gave a sly little smile. 'You're being replaced by new technology. A fully automated system. Like on the national lottery. The numbers will go up on a big screen and the computer will announce them.'

We couldn't believe our ears. Replacing us with a machine? 'The customers won't like it,' Julie said.

The Cobra shook his head. 'As long as they get their prizes, they wouldn't care if a talking monkey did the calling. Enjoy your last couple of weeks, ladies.' He turned away from us and started fiddling with his computer.

'You'll regret this,' Liz said defiantly.

'I don't think so,' he said, a sneer on his face. 'Oh, and another thing. This Children in Need night you're planning on Friday? Forget it. The Roxette is a business, not a charity. Friday night will be just like every other night.'

Well, that did it. We were even more outraged than we were on our own behalf. We'd been doing the Children in Need benefit night for nine years. All the winners donated their prizes, and Tyson Herbert donated a third of the night's takings. It was a big sacrifice all round, but we knew what hardship was, and we all wanted to do our bit.

'You bastard,' Julie said.

The Cobra swung round and glared at her. 'Would you rather be fired for gross misconduct, Julie? Walk out the door with no money and no reference? Because that's exactly what'll happen if you don't keep a civil tongue in your head.'

We hustled Julie out before she could make things worse. We were all fit to be tied, but we couldn't see any way of stopping the Cobra. I broke the news to Alan that teatime. Our Dickson had dropped in too – he's an actor now, he's got a part in one of the soaps, and they'd been doing some location filming locally. I don't know who was more angry, Alan or Dickson. After their tea, the two of them went down to the club full of fighting talk. But I knew it was just talk. There was nothing we could do against the likes of the Cobra.

I was as surprised as anybody when I heard about the armed robbery.

Keith

I don't know why I took this job. Everybody knows the Roxette's nothing but trouble. It's never turned the profit it should. And those bloody women. They made Tyson Herbert a laughing stock. But managers' jobs don't come up that often. Plus Head Office said they wanted the Roxette to become one of their flag-ship venues. And they wanted me to turn it around. Plus Margo's always on at me about Darren needing new this, new that, new the next thing. So how could I say no?

I knew as soon as I walked through the door it was going to be an uphill struggle. There was no sign of the new promo displays that Head Office was pushing throughout the chain. I eventually found them, still in their wrappers, in a cupboard in that pillock Herbert's office. I ask you, how can you drag a business into the twenty-first century if you're dealing with dinosaurs?

And the women. Everywhere, the women. You have to wonder what was going on in Herbert's head. It can't have been that he was dipping his wick, because they were all dogs. Apart from Julie. She was about the only one in the joint who didn't need surgical stockings. Not to mention plastic surgery. I might have considered keeping her on for a bit of light relief between houses. But she made it clear from the off that she had no fucking idea which side her bread was buttered. So she was for the chop like the rest of them.

I didn't hang about. I was right in there, making it clear who was in charge. I got the promo displays up on day one. Then I organised the delivery of the new computerised calling system. And that meant I could give the four calling birds the bullet sooner rather than later. That and knock their stupid charity stunt on the head. I ask you, who throws their profits down the drain like that in this day and age?

By the end of the first week, I was confident that I was all set. I had the decorators booked to bring the Roxette in line with the rest of the chain. Margo was pleased with the extra money in my wage packet, and even Darren had stopped whingeing.

I should have known better. I should have known it was all going too sweet. But not even in my wildest fucking nightmares could I have imagined how bad it could get.

By week two, I had my routines worked out. While the last house was in full swing, I'd do a cash collection from the front-of-house, the bar and the café. I'd bag it up in the office, ready for the bank in the morning, then put it in the safe overnight. And that's what I was doing on Wednesday night when the office door slammed open.

I looked up sharpish. I admit, I thought it was one of those bloody women come to do my head in. But it wasn't. At first, all I could take in was the barrel of a sawn-off shotgun, pointing straight at me. I nearly pissed myself. Instinctively I reached for the phone but the big fucker behind the gun just growled, 'Fucking leave it.' Then he kicked the door shut.

I dragged my eyes away from the gun and tried to get a look at him. But there wasn't much to see. Big black puffa jacket, jeans, black work boots. Baseball cap pulled down over his eyes, and a ski mask over the rest of his face. 'Keep your fucking mouth shut,' he said. He threw a black sports holdall towards me. 'Fill it up with the cash,' he said.

'I can't,' I said. 'It's in the safe. It's got a time lock.'

'Bollocks,' he said. He waved the gun at me, making me back up against the wall. What happened next was not what I expected. He grabbed the computer keyboard and pulled it across the desk. Then he turned the monitor round so it was facing him. With the hand that wasn't holding the gun, he did a few mouse clicks and then a bit of typing. I tried to edge out of his line of fire, but he wasn't having any. 'Fucking stand still,' he grunted.

Then he turned the screen back to face me and this time I nearly crapped myself. It was a live camera feed from my living room. Margo and Darren were huddled together on the sofa, eyes wide. Opposite them, his back to the camera, was another big fucker with a shotgun. The picture was a bit fuzzy and wobbly, but there was no mistake about it. Along the bottom of the picture, the seconds ticked away.

'My oppo's only a phone call away. Now are you going to fill the fucking holdall?' he demanded.

Well, I wasn't going to argue, was I? Not with my wife and kid facing a shooter. So I went to the safe. It hasn't got a time lock. Head Office wouldn't spend that kind of money. We're just told to say that to try and put off nutters like the big fucker who was facing me down in my own office. I was sweating so much my fingers were slipping off the keypad. But I managed it at the second go, and shovelled the bags of cash into his bag as fast as I could.

'Good boy,' he said when I'd finished.

I thought it was all over then. How wrong can you get?

'On your knees,' he ordered me. I didn't know what was going on. Part of me thought he was going to blow me away anyway. I was so fucking scared I could feel the tears in my eyes. I knew I was on the edge of losing it. Of begging him for my life. Only one thing stopped me. I just couldn't believe he was going to kill me. I mean, I know it happens. I know people get topped during robberies. But surely only if they put up a fight? And surely only when the robber is out of control? But the guy was totally calm. He could afford to be – his oppo's gun was still pointing straight at Margo and Darren.

So I fell to my knees.

Just thinking about what came next makes me retch. He dropped the gun to his side, at an angle so the barrel dug right into my gut. Then he unzipped his trousers and pulled out his cock. 'Suck my dick,' he said.

My head jerked back and I stared at him. I couldn't believe what I'd just heard. 'You what?'

'Suck my dick,' he said again, thrusting his hips towards me. His half-hard cock dangled in front of my face. It was the sickest thing I'd ever heard. It wasn't enough for this fucking pervert to terrorise my wife and kid and rob my safe. He wanted me to give him a blow job.

The gun jammed harder into me. 'Just fucking do it,' he said.

So I did.

He grabbed my hair and stopped me pulling back when I gagged. 'That's it. You know you want to,' he said softly, like this was something normal. Which it wasn't, not in any bloody sense.

It felt like it took a lifetime for him to come, but I suppose it was only a few minutes. When I felt his hot load hitting the back of my throat, I nearly bit his cock off in revulsion. But the gun in my chest and the thought of what might happen to Margo and Darren kept me inside the limits.

He stepped back, tucking himself away and zipping up. 'I enjoyed that,' he said.

I couldn't lift my head up. I felt sick to my stomach. And not just from what I'd swallowed either.

'Wait half an hour before you call the cops. We'll be watching, and if there's any funny business, your wife and kid get it, OK?' I nodded. I couldn't speak.

The last thing he did before he left was to help himself to the tape from the video surveillance system that is fed by the camera in my office. In a funny kind of way, I was almost relieved. I didn't want to think about that tape being played in the police station. Or in a courtroom, if it ever came to it.

So I did what I was told. I gave it thirty-five minutes, to be on the safe side. The police arrived like greased lightning. I thought things would get more normal then. Like *The Bill* or something. But it was my night for being well in the wrong. Because that's when things started to get seriously weird.

They'd sent a crew round to the house to check the robbers had kept their word and released Margo and Darren. They radioed back sounding pretty baffled. Turned out Margo was watching the telly and Darren was in his room playing computer games. According to them, that's what they'd been doing all evening. Apart from when Margo had been on the phone to her mate

Cheryl. Which had been more or less exactly when I'd supposedly been watching them being held hostage.

That's when the cops started giving me some very fucking funny looks. The boss, a DI Golightly, definitely wasn't living up to his name. 'So how did Chummy get in?' he demanded. 'There's no sign of forced entry at the back. And even though they were all eyes down inside the hall, I doubt they would have missed a six foot gunman walking through from the foyer.'

'I don't know,' I said. 'It should all have been locked up. The last person out would have been Liz Kirby. She called the session before the last one.'

By that time, they had the CCTV tapes of the car park. You could see the robber emerge from the shadows on the edge of the car park and walk up to the door. You couldn't see the gun, just the holdall. He opened the door without a moment's hesitation. So that fucking doozy Liz had left it unlocked.

'Looks like he walked straight in,' Golightly said. 'That was lucky for him, wasn't it?'

'I told you. It should have been locked. Look, I'm the victim here.'

He looked me up and down. 'So you say,' he said, sounding like he didn't believe a word of it. Then he wound the tape back further so we could see Liz leaving. And bugger me if she didn't turn around and lock the door behind her. 'How do you explain that?' he said.

All I could do was shrug helplessly.

He kept the digs and insinuations up for a while. He

obviously thought there was a chance I was in it up to my eyeballs. But there was fuck all proof so he had to let me go in the end. It had gone four in the morning by the time I got home. Margo was well pissed off. Apparently half the crescent had been glued to their windows after the flashing blue lights had alerted them that there was something more interesting than *Big Brother* going on outside their own front doors. 'I was black affronted,' Margo kept repeating. 'My family's never had the police at their door.' Like mine were a bunch of hardened criminals.

I didn't sleep much. Every time I got near to dropping off, I got flashbacks of that sick bastard's cock. I've never so much as touched another man's dick, not even when I was a kid. I almost wished I'd let the sad sack of shite shoot me.

Dickson

Everything I am, I owe to my mam. She taught me that I was as good as anybody else, that there was nothing I couldn't do if I wanted to. She also taught me the meaning of solidarity. Kick one, and we all limp. They should have that on the signs that tell drivers they're entering our town, right below the name of the Westphalian town we're twinned with.

So when she told me and my da what that prize prick Keith Corbett had planned for her and the other women at the Roxette, I was livid. And I was determined to do whatever I could to stop it happening. My mam and da have endured too bloody much already; they deserve not to have the rug pulled out from under them one more time.

After we'd had our tea, Da and I went down to the club. But I only stayed long enough to do some basic research. I had other fish to fry. I got on the mobile and arranged to meet up with Liz's daughters, Lauren and Shayla. Like me, they found a way out of the poverty trap that has our town between its teeth. They were always into computers, even at school. They both went to college and got qualifications in IT and now they run their own computer consultancy up in Newcastle. I had the germ of an idea, and I knew they'd help me make it a reality.

We met up in a nice little country pub over by Bishop Auckland. I told them what Corbett had in mind, and they were as angry as me. And when I laid out the bare bones of my plan, they were on board before I was half a dozen sentences into it. Right from the off, they were on side, coming up with their own ideas for making it even stronger and more foolproof.

It was Shayla who came up with the idea of getting Corbett to suck me off. At first, I was revolted. I thought it was grotesque. Over the top. Too cruel. I'll be honest, I've swung both ways in my time. Working in the theatre and telly, there's plenty of opportunities to explore the wilder shores of experience. But having a bit of fun with somebody you fancy is a far cry from letting some sleaze like Corbett anywhere near your tackle.

'I'd never be able to get it up,' I protested.

They both laughed. 'You're a bloke,' Lauren said dismissively. 'And you're an actor. Just imagine he's Jennifer Aniston.'

'Or Brad Pitt,' Shayla giggled.

'I think even Olivier might have had problems with that,' I sighed, knowing I was outgunned and outnumbered. It was clear to me now I'd brought them aboard, the two women were going to figure out a battle plan in which I was to be the foot soldier, the cannon fodder and the SAS all rolled into one.

The first – and most difficult – thing we had to do was to plant a fibre-optic camera in Corbett's lounge. We tossed around various ideas, all of which were both complicated and risky. Finally, Lauren hit on the answer. 'His lad's about twelve, thirteen, isn't he?' she asked.

I nodded. 'So I heard down the club.'

'That's sorted, then,' she said. 'I can get hold of some games that are at the beta-testing stage. We can knock up a letter telling Darren he's been chosen to test the games. Offer him a fee. Then I pick my moment, roll up at the house before he gets home. She's bound to invite me in and make me a cup of tea. I'll find somewhere to plant the camera and we're rolling.'

And that's exactly how it played out. Lauren got into the house, and while Margo Corbett was off making her a brew, she stuck the camera in the middle of a dried flower arrangement. Perfect.

The next phase was the most frustrating. We had to wait until we had the right set of pictures to make the scam work. For three nights, we filmed Corbett's living room, biting our nails, wondering how long it would take for mother and son to sit down together and watch something with enough dramatic tension. We cracked it on the Monday night when Channel Five was showing a horror movie. Darren and Margo sat next to each other, huddling closer as the climaxes piled up.

Then it was Shayla's turn. She spent the rest of Monday night and most of Tuesday putting together the short digital film that we would use to make sure Corbett did what he was told. Lauren had already filmed me against a blue background waving around the replica sawn-off shotgun we'd used as a prop last series. It hadn't been hard to liberate it from the props store. They're incredibly sloppy, those guys. Shayla cut the images in so it looked like I was standing in the Corbetts' living room threatening his nearest and dearest. I have to say, the end result was impressive and, more importantly, convincing.

Now we were ready. We chose Wednesday night to strike. Lauren had managed to get hold of her mam's keys and copied the one for the Roxette's back door. While the last session of the evening was in full swing, she'd slipped out and unlocked the door so I could walk straight in.

It all went better than I feared. You'd have thought Corbett was working from the same script, the way he caved in and did what he was told. And in spite of my fears, the girls had been right. My body didn't betray me.

I made my getaway without a problem and drove straight to Newcastle. Shayla got to work on the video, transferring it to digital, doing the edit and transferring it back to VHS tape again. I packed the money into a box and addressed it to Children in Need, ready to go in the post in the morning, then settled down to wait for Shayla.

The finished video was a masterpiece. We'd all been in Tyson Herbert's office for a drink at one time or another, so we knew where the video camera was. I'd been careful to keep my body between the camera and the gun for as much time as possible, which meant Shayla had been able to incorporate quite a lot of the original video. We had footage of Corbett packing the money into the holdall. Even better, we had the full blow job on tape without a single frame that showed the gun.

The final challenge was to deliver the video to Corbett without either the police or his wife knowing about it. In the end, we went for something we'd done on a stupid TV spy series I'd had a small part in a couple of years previously. We waited till he'd set off in the car, heading down the A1 towards our town. I followed him at a discreet distance then I called him on his mobile.

'Hello, Keith. This is your friend from last night.'

'You fucking cunt.'

'That's no way to speak to a man whose dick you've had in your mouth,' I said, going as menacing as I could manage. 'Listen to me. Three point four miles past the next exit, there's a lay-by. Pull over and take a look in the rubbish bin. You'll find something there that might interest you.' I cut the call and dialled Lauren. 'He's on his way,' I told her.

'OK, I'll make the drop.'

I came off the dual carriageway at the exit before the lay-by. I waited three minutes, then got back on the road. When I passed the lay-by, Corbett was standing by the bin, the padded envelope in his hand.

I sped past, then called him again. 'These are the edited highlights,' I told him. 'I'll call you in an hour when you've had the chance to check it out.'

He wasn't any happier when I made the call. 'You bastard,' he exploded. 'You total fucking bastard. You've made it look like we were in it together.'

'So we are, Keith,' I said calmly. 'You do something for me, and I won't send copies of the tape to the cops and your wife.'

'You blackmailing piece of shit,' he shouted.

'I'll take that as a yes, shall I?'

Noreen

You could have knocked me down with a feather. I didn't know what to expect when I turned up that Thursday for work, but it wasn't what happened. I knew about the robbery by then – the whole town was agog. I thought the Cobra would be pretty shaken up, but I didn't expect a complete personality change.

Before I'd even got my coat off, he was in the staff room, all smiles and gritted teeth. 'Noreen,' he said. 'A word, please?'

'How are you feeling, Mr Corbett?' I asked. 'That must have been a terrible experience.'

He looked away, almost as if he was ashamed. 'I don't want to discuss it.' He cleared his throat. 'Noreen, I might've been a bit hasty the other day. I've come to realise how much of the atmosphere at the Roxette depends on you and the girls.'

I couldn't believe my ears. I couldn't think of a single word to say. I just stood there with my mouth open.

'So, if you're willing to stay on, I'd like to offer you your job back.'

'What about the other girls? Liz and Jackie and Julie?' I couldn't have accepted if they weren't in the deal.

He nodded, although it looked as if the movement gave him pain. 'All four of you. Full reinstatement.'

'That's very generous of you,' I managed to say. Though what I really wanted was to ask him if he'd taken a blow to the head during the robbery.

He grimaced, his tight little face closed as a pithead. 'And if you still want to do the Children in Need night, we could make it next Friday,' he added, each word sounding like it was choked out of him.

'Thank you,' I said. I took a quick look out of the

window to see if there were any pigs flying past, but no. Whatever had happened inside the Cobra's head, the rest of the world seemed to be going on as normal.

And he was as good as his word. I don't know what changed his mind, but the four calling birds are back behind the balls at the Roxette. I still can't quite believe it, but as our Dickson reminded me, I've always said there's good in everybody. Sometimes, you just have to dig deep to find it.

Interview with Val McDermid

Where did you grow up?
I grew up in Fife, in Kirkcaldy and East Wemyss, in a working-class mining community.

Was yours a bookish household?
We didn't own books, but my parents both read. We lived opposite the town library, which is where I discovered the power of the written word.

Do you remember the first mystery novel you ever read?
The Murder at the Vicarage by Agatha Christie.

What was the first piece of music you recall?
'Scotland the Brave'. Mostly because I have a very early memory of Christmas in the town square where there was a machine into which you could insert two pennies and an array of plastic soldiers would march up and down to the tinny strains of 'Scotland the

Brave'. I also have very early memories of a Scottish lullaby called 'Dream Angus'.

Was yours a musically oriented household?
Yes. We listened to the radio a lot and always sang in the car. My father was a fine singer – he was the lead tenor in the concert party of the Bowhill People's Burns Club (Burns the poet, as opposed to the injury . . .) The decision as to which park we'd go to on a Sunday was always based on which silver or brass or pipe band was playing.

Do you listen to music when you write?
Invariably.

The Long Black Veil was inspired by the song of the same name, which you perform on stage with the Fun Lovin' Crime Writers band. Have any other musical works ever inspired a novel or short story?
My father used to sing a song called 'The Road and the Mile to Dundee' – it was his signature piece. I wrote a story about it a couple of years ago, which is included in *Stranded*, my short story collection. And one of my novels, *The Distant Echo*, takes its title from a quote from a Jam song, 'Down in the Tube Station at Midnight'. Though the book itself owes more to a Deacon Blue song called 'Orphans' . . .

What is your favourite man-made sound?
My child's voice.

What is your favourite sound in nature?
The sea on the shore.

If you had to choose three novels to take on a trip, what would you choose?
Robert Louis Stevenson's *Treasure Island*; Jeanette Winterson's *The Passion*; Reginald Hill's *On Beulah Height*.

How do you start a story?
With a small, often tangential fact or anecdote that sets the bells ringing inside my head. It has to be exciting, it has to clamour at the doors of my imagination. Then I play 'what if' with it and find out whose story it is. Then I start to push and pull it in different directions till it starts to feel like a story.

If you had a chance to invite any three people in the world to dinner, living or dead, who would they be?
Robert Louis Stevenson, Joni Mitchell and Christopher Marlowe.

Which would you rather do – read or listen to a favourite CD?
Both. I like to have music on while I read.

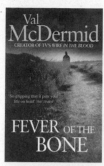

Val **McDermid**
CREATOR OF TV'S *WIRE IN THE BLOOD*

'So gripping that it puts your life on hold' *THE TIMES*

FEVER OF THE BONE

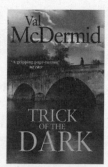

Val **McDermid**

'A gripping page-turner' *METRO*

TRICK OF THE DARK

Val **McDermid**
CREATOR OF TV'S *WIRE IN THE BLOOD*

'Stunningly good'

THE RETRIBUTION

Val **McDermid**

'A genuine page-turner' *Independent on Sunday*

It's every parent's worst nightmare . . .

THE VANISHING POINT

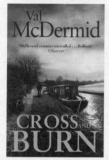

Val **McDermid**

'McDermid remains unrivalled . . . Brilliant' *Observer*

CROSS AND BURN

Val **McDermid**
THE SUNDAY TIMES NUMBER ONE BESTSELLER

'The real mistress of psychological gripping thrillers: no one can plot or tell a story like she can' *Daily Express*

THE SKELETON ROAD

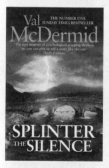

Val **McDermid**
THE NUMBER ONE SUNDAY TIMES BESTSELLER

'The real mistress of psychological gripping thrillers: no one can plot or tell a story like she can' *Daily Express*

SPLINTER THE SILENCE

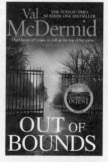

Val **McDermid**
THE SUNDAY TIMES NUMBER ONE BESTSELLER

'The Queen of Crime is still at the top of her game'

OUT OF BOUNDS

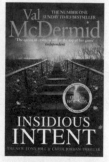

Val **McDermid**
THE NUMBER ONE SUNDAY TIMES BESTSELLER

'The queen of crime is still at the top of her game' *Independent*

INSIDIOUS INTENT

THE NEW TONY HILL & CAROL JORDAN THRILLER

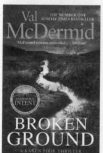

Val **McDermid**
THE NUMBER ONE SUNDAY TIMES BESTSELLER

'McDermid remains unrivalled . . . Brilliant'

BROKEN GROUND

A KAREN PIRIE THRILLER

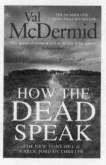

Val **McDermid**
THE NUMBER ONE SUNDAY TIMES BESTSELLER

'The queen of crime is still at the top of her game' *Independent*

HOW THE DEAD SPEAK

THE NEW TONY HILL & CAROL JORDAN THRILLER

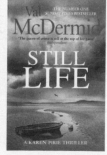

Val **McDermid**
THE NUMBER ONE SUNDAY TIMES BESTSELLER

'The queen of crime is still at the top of her game' *Independent*

STILL LIFE

A KAREN PIRIE THRILLER

DON'T MISS THE
ALLIE BURNS SERIES

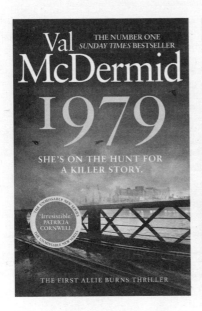
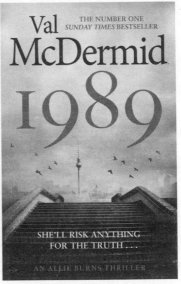

'A supremo of the genre at the height of her
powers ... An unmissable new series'
Peter James

OUT NOW